# THE BIG BET

## Payment in Kind

Owen B. Greenwald

**EPIC**
Press

Payment in Kind
The Big Bet: Book #4

Written by Owen B. Greenwald

Copyright © 2016 by Abdo Consulting Group, Inc.

Published by EPIC Press™
PO Box 398166
Minneapolis, MN 55439

Cover design by Candice Keimig
Images for cover art obtained from iStockPhoto.com
Edited by Ryan Hume

LIBRARY OF CONGRESS CATALOGING-IN-PUBLICATION DATA

Greenwald, Owen B.
Payment in kind / Owen B. Greenwald.
p. cm. — (The big bet ; #4)
Summary: Jason and the team head back to Las Vegas to track down whoever gave
them the basketball job and set them on their current, failed path. In desperation,
Jason turns to an old friend and former CPC member, Z Davis. But whether he
actually wants to help them is another matter.
ISBN 978-1-68076-186-3 (hardcover)
1. Swindlers and swindling—Fiction. 2. Deception—Fiction. 3. Young adult
fiction. I. Title.
[Fic]—dc23
2015949057

EPIC
Press

*For the friends who supported me along the way, encouraged me, and understood my limitations, from the Bay Area to Providence to Fir Acres and many other places besides.*
*And for Brandon Sanderson, who will never know how much his books inspired me to write.*

# ONE

WE MET IN GRAND CENTRAL STATION, SHE and I.

She was perhaps five years my senior and pretty, with dark auburn hair, a heart-shaped face, and what Lucas, with a hearty guffaw, would call *child-bearing hips*. Her large brown eyes peeked out inquisitively behind long lashes as she looked me over.

And she could probably kill me in a dozen different ways before I could shout for help.

I was gambling that meeting in such a public location would make such an outcome unlikely, but you never know. I'd also poached some of the

Applewoods' security detail and scattered them among the crowd, knowing that realistically, they'd be fast enough to avenge my untimely end and not much else.

"You are Jason Jorgensen?" she asked, dispelling any lingering doubts that she wasn't who I was here to meet. She *was* wearing the indigo feather I'd been told to look for . . . but I'd been expecting someone else.

"That's me," I said. "And you're not Lorenzo Michaelis."

After all the trouble I'd gone to arranging this meeting, the least the street boss of the New York Mafia's Bonanno family could've done was to show up himself—not that we were on good terms at the moment. Just two days ago, I'd been spearheading a campaign against his entire organization . . . before it'd gone disastrously wrong. I'd been coping with the fallout ever since.

No time to mourn, no time to rest. I *had* to meet with them before they could strike again, while I could negotiate from a position of relative advantage. I felt *ragged*, hounded on all sides. What I *really* wanted was to bask in the afterglow of the kiss Addie and I'd shared, but every second we were still fighting the Mafia was another second Lorenzo could order another attack.

My first step'd been to safeguard our homes. Lucas kept a file of . . . let's call them *independent contractors* . . . he considered both reliable and trustworthy (I wasn't supposed to know about it, but that'd never stopped me before). From it, I'd selected a team of bodyguards-for-hire led by a man named Derek. Derek was an impressive figure—ex-special forces with a resume longer than my forearm, containing jobs both legal and otherwise, and he and his twelve-person team were now deployed around-the-clock at Kira's, Addie's, and yes, even Z's houses. Even if negotiations succeeded today, I planned on keeping them on—trusting the Mafia's word is a good way to end up dead. And there was no particular cost associated with their continued service, besides their salary . . . which, while admittedly steep, was being paid out of one of Lucas's overseas accounts. I doubted he'd notice.

But they wouldn't be enough if the Mafia launched another dedicated attack. We *needed* something more stable—peace.

Luckily, so did they.

"*Il Diavoletto* has many enemies," said the woman coolly. "He would not meet you here— not without knowing it would be safe."

"But you have leave to speak for him?"

"I do."

It would've been remiss to arrange this meeting without doing my research, and what information I'd been able to uncover without Z's help indicated that I was speaking to one of Lorenzo's *valchiria*— specially trained bodyguards, all women, whose skills he was known to boast about to anyone who would listen. He was quite paranoid—a healthy trait for a mob boss—but he trusted his *valchiria* more than most. It was perfectly in character for him to send one instead of exposing himself to assassins.

Still, I'd been prepared to deal with *him*. This woman was an unknown entity.

"Then let's talk."

I took a step closer, out from under the massive, intricately decorated dome in the center of the room. We were relying on the ambient noise of countless commuters to mask our discussion, but a little extra caution never hurt.

"I'm here to propose a cessation of hostilities," I said. Just forcing the words out felt like surrender, but they had to be said. As long as the Mafia knew my identity, continuing the fight even one day longer was too dangerous.

Amid the tumult, I'd found time to wonder how they *had* found us. I'd been careful—we all had. What'd gone wrong?

The mystery'd flummoxed me until I'd happened upon a key piece of information. Stephen

Lister, the Van Buren teacher who'd overheard us plotting, had a brother in the NYPD. And while I didn't have any *proof*, it wasn't hard to connect the dots.

Maybe I could expose him somehow. Even if I couldn't, there were other ways to get him off the force. New York deserved better than a compromised police division.

The *valchiria* tossed her head scornfully, bringing me back to the present. "In your arrogance, you thought you could attack us without worry. Now that we have responded, you hasten to grovel for forgiveness. The Mafia does not let their enemies walk free, Mr. Jorgensen, no matter how frightened they are."

"Ah, yes." I kept my tone casual, trying not to betray my flash of anger that she was *right*. "Your *response*. Losing four teams—fourteen men total—for one man who was not even the primary target. A few more victories like that and you'll be out of members."

Her eyes darkened, and she suddenly looked uncannily like Kira.

I pressed my advantage—they should've sent a better negotiator. "And the man you *did* shoot? I suspect Lorenzo's not too happy about that. The police aren't happy about the death of one of their own, I've heard. You must've heard the same."

I felt a twinge of guilt as I remembered Z's grief-torn face as he accused me of engineering a movement against the Mafia by law enforcement. I hadn't even *considered* doing anything of the sort—but that didn't make the fact that it was happening less true.

And no matter what Z thought, it was an opening I *had* to take advantage of. It was everything I'd been hoping for, just at the cost of one precious life . . . and one friendship.

"If it's war you want, we'll oblige," I said. "But you don't wanna fight us *and* the law at the same time. That's a fight you won't win."

I knew she wouldn't admit I was right, but she

didn't have to. The facts were on my side, and Lorenzo was smart enough to read them as I had. This *valchiria* had one job, and that was to accept my offer without losing the Bonannos more face than they had lost already.

"And what terms are you willing to offer?"

"I and my associates will not interfere with the operations of the Bonannos, or any other Mafia family, in any way. Neither will we hire nor incite other groups to do so, or compete with Mafia operations. We offer complete peace . . . and will take nothing less in return."

The *valchiria* considered. "In exchange, *Il Diavoletto* is willing to forget the insult you have offered his family. It will no longer earn you our enmity going forward. However . . . future crimes will not be similarly protected. Break your word, and we will see you punished all the more harshly for its breaking."

There were loopholes, no denying that. But this woman was no lawyer, and I couldn't imagine

Lorenzo exploiting the letter of the law—he'd either break the spirit or keep it, and insisting on a more careful wording wouldn't change anything. On the surface, this was exactly what I'd been looking for.

"I understand, and I accept your terms."

Slowly, she extended a hand to shake. I didn't take it—the stories of Lorenzo's negotiators wearing barbed rings tipped with slow-acting poison were warning enough.

"My word will have to suffice."

For a moment I thought she was going to insist, but she just gave me a measured, calculating look. I thought I caught a glimmer of respect from behind her lashes.

"It is done," she said. And the CPC was safe again, for the immediate future.

Then she walked past me, into the teeming throng of Grand Central, and disappeared.

# TWO

FOR MANY HIGH SCHOOLERS, GRADUATION'S A culminating experience—the sum total of four years of hard work, a transition point between childhood and responsibility, a chance to leave the parts of you that you never liked behind as you step forward into the rest of your life.

Many high schoolers haven't rigged sporting events, cheated businessmen out of millions of dollars, and tussled with the Italian Mafia. That's to say, they aren't me—or one of the (almost) equally-talented operatives at my beck and call.

Once you've gone through what we have—grown

up several times over—graduation's just a day full of irrelevant traditions and blowhards convincing themselves they're important. They're hours that could be used for more important things—plotting, for example.

So you shouldn't be surprised that that's exactly what my two teammates and I were using it for. We were scheduled to walk on stage with the rest of the seniors any time now, but we'd huddled together in a corner, determined to make every last minute count. We sat well apart from everyone else, discussing business in low whispers. Nobody gave us a second glance—this kind of behavior was expected of us by now.

The flipside of that was, we were now recognizable enough that things were expected of us. In our business, it's always best to stay inconspicuous, and until recently, we'd been doing pretty well. Unfortunately, being involved in a highly publicized local news story about the Mafia's resurgence gets you *noticed*. It'd been impossible to circumvent—once the school discovered our families'd been at the epicenter of the first round of attacks, there was no escape. We'd spent the next month trying to drive home the message that we didn't wanna discuss it. Finally, they'd figured it out and left us alone, only now we had this reputation as the weird kids who only talked to each other because of our shared trauma.

And if anyone thought it was strange that we weren't closer friends with the fourth student affected, the one who'd *actually* lost a parent, who was friends with pretty much *everybody* . . . well, they didn't ask *us* about it.

Seeing Z was awkward when we happened to pass him in the hallways. He always walked right by, staring straight ahead, holding his expression in a frozen mask until we'd passed each other. In class, he avoided my eyes. In about twenty minutes, he'd be on stage with us as we graduated, but you can bet he wouldn't look our way once. And then the three of us would party at a restaurant, and he'd . . . well, he'd have no shortage of people to celebrate with, but that wasn't the point.

He belonged with *us*.

We'd talked once—just once—about the possibility of convincing him to return. The discussion'd started out reasonable enough, albeit nobody had any actual good ideas. Then I'd made the mistake of suggesting Kira use her feminine wiles. Kira'd had a coughing fit from laughing too hard, and then explained how many pieces she'd divide my body into if I suggested anything like that ever again. And since that'd actually been my number one idea, the discussion'd ended there. Nobody seemed keen to revisit it.

Instead, we made do with three team members instead of four. And while none of us could ever match the utility Z'd brought with his vast network of contacts (or "friends" as he'd called them), we also operated on a much smaller scale than we had as a four-person team. Gone were the days of rigging NCAA basketball games or cheating

high-rollers at the poker table. The largest operation we'd pulled since the truce with the Mafia was
cornering the Van Buren answer key black market,
which, though it *did* pay out reliably every week,
was about as challenging as teaching an eighth-
grader to play rock-paper-scissors.

The three of us were in agreement—we needed
to do something big to celebrate our liberation
from adolescent hell. The catch? That *something*
looked different to each of us.

"No, it's not *actually* a protection racket. It's
just gotta *look* like a protection racket long enough
to get our hands on the cash."

Currently, Kira was defending her brainchild—
and lemme tell you, there's a reason she usually
sticks to computers.

"What you're describing is *literally* a protection
racket," said Addie. "If you tell someone to give
you ten dollars or you'll break their kneecaps, the
effect is the same whether you're planning on following through or not. It doesn't matter that we're

going to disappear after the first payment, it still counts."

"Okay, fine, so it's a protection racket. Whatever."

"No, *not* whatever," Addie said firmly. "Protection rackets are the mob's deal. I don't want it to look like we're trying to muscle in on their territory. Especially not now."

That shut Kira up.

"But do you know what the mob *doesn't* do?" Addie continued. "Bank heists. Good, old-fashioned bank heists."

"Yeah, and there's a reason they don't," I said. "For every high-profile success, hundreds end with the robbers in prison. You just can't get away with it anymore."

Addie winked at me. "What, are you saying the great Jason Jorgensen isn't up for the challenge?"

Ooh. Playing off my ego. Well, there was no rule that said she had to fight fair, even if—and she'd argue, *especially since*—we were dating. But two could play at that game.

"Part of making plans is knowing what *won't* work. And without someone with an inside connection at the bank, that's everything."

*Someone with an inside connection.* In our personal group language, that straight-up translated to *Z*.

The moment I alluded to our one-time fourth member, the atmosphere of the conversation darkened, and Addie let the subject drop. Nobody wanted to dwell on the hole in our team. I'd probably get some shit later for bringing it up.

But honestly? As bad as I felt for what'd happened to Hector, Z was riding the blame train *way* too fucking hard. My plan'd *worked*. I hadn't told him to run upstairs and get shot. If he'd stayed put like I'd intended, everything would've been *fine*.

It was hard to blame Z for being mad given what he'd been through . . . but somehow, I managed.

"I've been thinking," I began, then paused in

case Kira wanted to say "about time," or something similar. But the specter of Z's absence still hung over our heads, and my comment passed unembroidered. "About this hypothetical big job. We've pulled off some incredible shit before. We've made truckloads of cash before, too. Is doing those things again really that special? The crown jewel of our high school career?"

"He's doing it again," said Kira. "Asking leading questions."

"The point is that we're in a rut and we need to get out of it," said Addie. "We aren't reinventing the wheel here."

I pulled out my phone and started flipping through old pictures. "Right. We *are* in a rut. We lost a lot of money and twenty-five percent of the team in a spat with the mob, and we're still hurting. We've gone from Robert Downey Jr. to Nicholas Cage. And where'd our problems start? The Vegas job."

With a theatrical flourish, I placed my phone

in the center of our makeshift circle. Displayed onscreen was a blurry picture of a large man, snapped at an awkward angle.

"You remember this man, I hope. He paid us fifty thousand each to come to Vegas and rig the game, but he didn't reveal his employer. In hindsight, that should've been a warning sign."

I thought back to the cold spike of fear as our executioner pointed his gun at us, and the knowledge that I had no more tricks up my sleeve, no cards left to play. It didn't take much to bring that old terror to the surface—I'd remember it until the day I died. That was what *losing* felt like.

And I never wanted to feel it again.

"You might also remember that the Mafia claimed they paid us nothing. That's two hundred thousand dollars unaccounted for. Where'd it come from? I bet this man knows the answer." I tapped the screen casually.

"Jason, we have a truce with the mob. It's *over.*

The way you're talking doesn't sound like truce-talk to me."

Addie tends to be the team's voice of reason, which is handy, because we need at least *one*. I'll be the first to admit I can let vision overrule logistics, and Kira, well . . . Kira would swan dive into a volcano if you told her it'd challenged her to a fight.

At least, that *used* to be true. Now I wasn't sure what was up with her. She'd been acting weird and pacifist-y since Vegas until the day of the mob raid. On that day, I'd asked her straight-up if she was willing to fight, and she'd said she was.

If only it were that simple. According to her, she'd driven off the hit men sent to Addie's house with no trouble—but when she'd said that, all of Addie's bullshit-o-meters went off. Addie's kinda like a human polygraph, except I actually trust her.

So we'd investigated. Addie'd asked her mom what'd happened that day, and I'd looked through a few news reports, swallowing my discomfort the whole time. What she and I had learned aligned—the team dispatched to Addie's house hadn't even *made* it to Kira. They'd argued among each other for some unknown reason and three'd ended up dead before the fourth fled the scene.

I dunno why Kira couldn't just *tell* us that, but maybe she was ashamed she hadn't stopped them herself. Maybe she'd hid instead of fighting them like she promised or something—she'd see that as displaying weakness and try and cover it up as much as possible. Neither of us thought it was worth calling her out, though, so maybe we'd never know exactly what'd happened. Everything'd turned out alright—that's what *really* mattered.

Instead, I'd adapted—recalibrated my priors for what tasks Kira could reliably take on. But I'd done so prematurely, because just a couple weeks later, Kira was back to her old, punch-happy self—if not *more* so. She'd taken up boxing and was the favorite to win regionals later this month.

"We have a truce with the *mob*, yes," I admitted.

"But I'm starting to wonder if this mystery man has anything to do with them. Nothing wrong with digging a little—we don't have to commit to anything until we know more. Whatever he was up to, it screwed us big time. Enough that it deserves an investigation. Right?"

Addie looked unsure. "And why are you saying all this now? I *know* you didn't put this together last night . . . "

"Well, no, because last night we were—"

Kira coughed loudly.

"Right, well. We've all had lots to think about, and I figured the longer we waited, the less likely he'd be to expect us. False sense of security and all that."

It was clear that neither Kira nor Addie believed me; Addie was giving me a particularly suspicious look. I sighed.

"It's not like I was saving this plan for graduation day because it means we have an excuse to celebrate in Las Vegas . . . "

I let my voice trail off tantalizingly, and was rewarded with a bright grin from Kira. "I think I could get behind this plan."

"Is there any reason to start our search there?" asked Addie, ever the voice of reason. "For all we know, he could live in Florida—or two blocks from here."

Ever since I'd gotten the idea of tracking him down, the problem of *where to start looking* had been percolating in my brain. How do you locate someone you only met briefly, using only a single blurry photograph? If you're as smart as I am, the first step's understanding that said photograph's hardly your only asset. You have dozens of little clues from that brief meeting, waiting to be discovered and applied, if you only scrutinize your memory. And I had. Painstakingly.

"He's not from here," I said. "At least, it's not likely. Z didn't know him. And nobody Z knows knew him either. So either he's not a New Yorker, or he's a goddamned hermit. Now, why Las Vegas? First off, he knew the mob there was hiring. That means he has connections in the city, so even if he isn't native himself, there's probably someone there who knows where to find him. Second, you said he talked like a west-coaster."

"I'm surprised you remembered that," said Addie. "Now you have no excuse if you forget our anniversary."

I didn't see a reason to mention I'd put the date into a reminder app the day we made things official. The wise are never unprepared.

"Third, well . . . Vegas. Us, newly graduated. The plan writes itself."

"Teacher," muttered Addie in a monotone, and we quieted at once. Sure enough, Ms. Rosenbaum was pushing her way toward us, gesturing toward the stage. It was time.

"Think about it," I said, ignoring my protesting knees as I stood. "See you on the other side."

I gave Addie a quick kiss, then drifted off to join the other Js. The time had come to put high school behind me. Forever.

# THREE

DIDN'T BOTHER TELLING LUCAS I WAS LEAVING. I doubted he'd care.

I *did* leave a note explaining I'd be gone for about a week. In case he didn't see it, I also told Jeeves.

Hell, he was probably *relieved* I was gone. He'd said more than once he expected me to have my own place the day I graduated. Probably would've already kicked me out, but I think he'd forgotten about my graduation. He hadn't been there, anyway—though Jeeves had, and he'd congratulated me stiffly after the ceremony concluded.

Jeeves has always been at least *decent* to me,

even if he's sometimes annoying as hell. Besides, I can't trust him—I just *know* everything I tell him gets back to Lucas. Still, I sometimes think that if I'd been a duller, more boring, dutiful son, Jeeves would've made a good substitute father for the neglectful giant I'd been saddled with.

But I wasn't, he wasn't, and we weren't. And that was that.

Point is, out of us three, I had it easiest selling the "celebration trip to Las Vegas" angle to my parents. Not that anyone had much trouble—after all, we'd already been earlier this year. Everything'd gone smoothly and safely *last* time, so why would they worry?

Well, smoothly and safely except when we were driven into the desert and almost shot dead. But nobody's parents knew about that part (I hope. And if they did, I imagine our "group trip to Las Vegas" proposal would've been much less successful).

The flight'd been uneventful, and as pleasant as possible being crammed into a metal tube

and squashed between two other equally inconvenienced—and therefore irritable—passengers
for six hours. Which is to say, one of those two
people was Addie. Using our cramped quarters as
an excuse for cuddling *almost* made having Kira
on my other side tolerable. Unfortunately, Kira's
sensitive about her personal space. She's also in
possession of two unbelievably sharp elbows and
prefers physical solutions over talking things out.
As you can imagine, these traits don't combine
well—particularly on an aircraft.

I spent most of the flight staring at the middle-
man's picture and trying to glean clues from his
various physical traits, but without much success.
I could generalize *somewhat*—the buzz cut could
indicate a relation to the military, while his outfit
hinted at a familiarity with fine clothes. But there
was nothing like a name tag, or a mysterious tattoo
of a symbol covered recently in the front-page
news as belonging to a specific and well-known
cult. And inaccurate generalizations could only

get an investigation so far before it started actually *impeding* the effort.

The rest was spent on the Frame. We had only a vacation's worth of time to accomplish our task, so taking a few days to "settle in" (code for "give the planner time to actually do his job") could separate success from failure.

The plans were all very different and very wild. My early plans tend that way before I start culling the herd and fleshing out the survivors. The only similarities this early crop shared were the first two steps, which went something like this.

Step one—tap Z's contacts for anyone who might know our mystery man.

Followed invariably by step two—oh, right.

None of them'd managed to grow large enough to break away from the pack by the time we began our descent, so I resigned myself to letting everyone but me take several days to "settle in".

I gave a loud, relieved sigh as the plane touched the runway—a sigh I immediately regretted as I remembered my internal resolution never to set foot in Las Vegas again. In New York, it'd been easy to let the glitz and glamor drift to the forefront of my memory while the seediness faded to the back, but just landing at McCarren Airport was enough to bring it all back.

Still, if my options were the city of Las Vegas and a seat on an airplane next to Kira, queen of pointy extremities, I'd take the former ten times out of ten. Leave it to my subconscious to construct a plan that would make me *eager* to set foot in Nevada.

"We renting?" asked Kira as the plane parked by the terminal. People sprang up like fast-growing weeds, clogging the aisle. I chose to remain seated—no sense in standing awkwardly for five minutes waiting for the traffic jam to dissolve. *Christ*, I missed having enough cash to fly first class. Answer-key money could be stretched only so far. But the barbaric conditions—the square inch of legroom, the one bathroom per hundred people, the seats that might as well've been cushioned with cardboard—made me wish I'd sprung for it anyway.

And while I'm sure this isn't a common complaint, opening up the in-flight magazine and seeing a big *Jorgensen International* ad splayed across two pages hadn't done wonders for my mood either.

"Huh?

"You know, how are we getting around?"

"You need to be twenty-five to rent a car," Addie pointed out.

"Unfortunately, we fell victim to a classic teenage blunder—nobody thinks about renting a car when they commission their fakes," I said. "Not that we could've gotten away with it. Twenty-five's harder to pull off than twenty-one."

"They're both easy," grinned Addie. "The proportions are a little wonky, but I'd make it work."

"So yeah, probably just taxis then," I said, taking us back to the original subject. "We're low on cash though, so try to make every trip count."

Kira looked a little put out that she wouldn't get to drive all vacation, but what choice did she have? If she wanted to drive so bad, she could buy her own damn car.

. . . Actually, considering current taxi fares, that might be a better deal.

The line of passengers slowly evaporated and I stood as its front neared our position. I never understood airplane seating. To me, the obvious thing to do would be to load the *back* of the plane first rather than the front, also staggering in some window seat-ers in the earlier rows. Then just move forward, filling in the rest. But god forbid the first class passengers board a *little* later than the peasants. Like boarding first's some sacred honor.

After what felt like years, we finally made our way to the front of the plane and escaped into the airport proper, where we were greeted by beeping slot machines the second we stepped out of the gate.

They don't waste any time hooking you on

gambling in Nevada—as soon as you land at McCarren, you can start pissing your savings away. Gotta wring those last few dollars out of the tourists before they leave. There were machine clusters *everywhere*, and no cluster was entirely unattended.

"What's the plan?" Addie asked faux-innocently as we strolled past the last of the "C" gates, trailing our luggage. Subtle as it was, her reproach came across clear as day—she might as well've pointed an accusing finger right in my face and screamed, *Why don't you have a plan yet, dumbass?*

I'd known this moment would be coming, but I still had no way to sugarcoat it. "We're dead in the water without Z. We need his connections, and the one guy we know he's friends with is in the Mafia. I don't feel like gambling that the Bonanno family's Vegas branch is clueless about what we did to their pals in New York—besides, even if they aren't, they're supposed to think we're dead. Either way, we aren't engaging with them at all this trip. That leaves us with, lemme count . . . no leads."

Addie smiled triumphantly and held out an open palm to Kira, who growled and handed her a twenty.

"You took *bets?*" I said, horrified. And then, "You *bet against me?*"

"I'm *really* let down, boss," said Kira dejectedly. "I believed in you."

"Nothing personal," Addie explained. "It's the risk-averse maneuver. Either we have a working plan, or I get paid. Win-win."

"She doesn't get that it's actually lose-lose," said Kira.

"Babe?" said Addie, "That flight *sucked.*"

I could tell where she was going with this, and even worse, I knew she was right.

"Three thousand miles of low-grade inconvenience so we can sit on our hands without any direction? What if planning the operation takes you the full week, and we have to fly home before we can implement it? As much fun as vacations are, we *did* come here for a reason."

"I thought I could come up with something on the plane," I said tiredly. "And I did. I came up with all sorts of things—they just all sucked. Unless you *want* to call every name in Nevada's white pages until you recognize a voice, or create a fake online dating profile with an *incredibly* specific "looking for" section . . . "

Addie and Kira looked almost ashamed on my behalf.

"You're used to hearing my *good* ideas," I explained. "I think up *shit-tons* of awful ones that never see daylight. This time was especially tough because I had to rule out everything that cost too much. The best idea I had was filing a false missing person's report, but I decided it could backfire too easily."

"At least you tried," sighed Addie. But the frost in her bearing refused to melt.

We made contact with a taxi driver outside the airport and were soon headed back to fabulous Las Vegas. Only this time, instead of being alone with nothing to do but contemplate the dreariness of the landscape, I was racking my brain for avenues I hadn't yet explored.

"Z would make this so *easy*," I snapped, when my attempts proved fruitless. "He'd know a guy, or a guy who knows a guy, and we'd get started. The only people *we* know here hate us."

I was thinking mostly about Isaiah Porter, the basketball referee we'd blackmailed last time we were in the city—not that he'd have been any help whatsoever.

I'd almost reached the point where *calling* Z and asking for help became tempting. Play the *favor to an old friend* angle. Or maybe get Addie to do it, since Z had a special problem with *me* in particular. But he'd laugh in our faces either way—I knew he would. And yet . . . could there really be any harm in *asking*? It's not like the favor was particularly large—give me as little as five minutes' access to his network of friends and I could crack this puzzle wide open.

And then I noticed the implication of what I'd just thought and cursed myself for not having seen it earlier.

"I got it," I said triumphantly. "The plan. And technically, we haven't entered the city of Las Vegas yet, so . . . "

I waggled my eyebrows hopefully at Addie, who couldn't stifle a small, amused smile. Well, she *could*, but . . .

"Alright, I'll let you off the hook *this* time," she teased. "What's the angle?"

"It's not *Z* we need," I explained. "It's the people he knows. So if we can find *them* . . . "

**FOUR**

"HOLY SHIT," KIRA HISSED LOUDLY. "WHAT happened to his shirt?"

I blinked, rubbed my eyes, then looked back at the bare-chested, handsome man on stage, who'd definitely been wearing a shirt when his act began. He kept up a steady stream of patter as he rifled through a deck of cards, seemingly unconcerned he'd lost half his wardrobe.

"It was Velcro-ed together from the front," Addie whispered. "When everyone was looking at the volunteer, he ripped it off and tossed it behind the armchair. You didn't see that?"

I certainly hadn't. "Magic Miles," as he was

billed, was obviously both naturally talented and well-practiced. It was your traditional stage magician act, only with an element of stripping involved. He'd tossed his hat into the crowd near the beginning, followed shortly by his coat. Now he was down to his red necktie, his trousers, and whatever was underneath.

He flashed a charming smile at his audience as his current trick neared its conclusion.

"As you can see, nothing up my sleeves . . . including my sleeves," he joked, indicating his newly-bare arms. "Now we're gonna shuffle this deck a little more until you're all good and satisfied, alright?"

Addie rolled her eyes. "The card isn't even in the deck, it's behind him. He tucked it there before he started shuffling."

"I'm never taking you to a magic show again," I admonished. She'd been saying shit like that the whole time.

Magic Miles, now holding and shuffling the deck with one hand, held up his other in a "stop" motion with a showman's flourish. "I can see it in your faces, you're suspicious. If I'm really shuffling, why am I looking at the deck so closely? That is a *wonderful* question—give yourselves a hand!"

The audience clapped obediently.

"And to address your concerns, I will continue to shuffle the deck . . . blindfolded. Alec, do the honors, please!"

Magic Miles' laconic assistant stepped forward as Magic Miles himself undid his necktie to loud cheers of encouragement—including a whoop from Kira. He only had one hand to work at the knot with, but it still lasted only seconds beneath his well-practiced fingers. Alec took the loose necktie and bound it securely around Miles' eyes.

"Hmmm," said Miles. "This is making it *pretty* tough to shuffle, I admit. But I'm a pro, I know what I'm doing, and so I'll have to make this a little harder on myself. Now, some magicians will perform their tricks blindfolded. Some will perform their tricks with their hands behind their backs. But

I, Magic Miles, am the only magician who has ever gone so far as to do both . . . at the same time!"

And so saying, he put his hands behind his back.

"Told you," said Addie smugly.

Slowly, Magic Miles rotated around to face away from us. We could see him shuffling, but if Addie was right—and she probably was—he'd already grabbed the card out of his belt. He'd started turning as soon as his hands went behind him, and if Addie hadn't said anything earlier, I never would've noticed.

Now's probably a good time to explain why I was watching a stage magician strip down to his boxers. See, "Magic Miles" was actually a friend of Z's named Miles Dutch, and I was hoping he'd help us if we namedropped our old friend to him. Miles couldn't possibly know we weren't currently on speaking terms, right?

I'd realized in the taxi that I had access to a list of people Z knew—his Facebook profile. He'd blocked me and Addie when he quit the CPC, but he hadn't extended the same insult to Kira (Kira thought he was being lazy. Neither Addie nor I corrected her). So we'd logged on to her account, clicked over to Z's page, and pulled up his friends list.

It would've taken forever to search through Z's innumerable Facebook friends until we found one from Las Vegas, much less one who might be helpful. So instead, we worked it from the other direction— spent an afternoon looking up various casinos' entertainers and searching their names in the list.

Casino entertainers were our first line of attack. The Mafia'd once had financial ties to most of Las Vegas's casinos, but those days were mostly over. The capos adapted to law enforcement's pressure by "adopting" the tertiary businesses *supplying* the casinos—all the profit, and none of the scrutiny. Actual casino employees were about as close as you could get to Vegas's criminal element without actually rubbing up against them, and the few employees whose names were public record—even *advertised*—were the entertainers. Miles Dutch was the third name we'd tried, and he'd popped right up.

He was currently employed at New York, New York, which we'd unanimously agreed was symbolically appropriate. And so we'd come to pay him a visit, but it was only polite to suffer through the crowds and ever-present stench of cigarettes to watch his act before we started asking him favors.

Or so Kira and Addie had argued, at least.

"Be right back—bathroom," said Addie, and slipped effortlessly through the tightly-packed crowd. Onstage, Miles was having his wrists cinched with his own belt. By the time she returned, he was dangling upside-down from a crossbar, having his stomach lightly tickled by an enthusiastic volunteer—and still shuffling that same deck.

"Pretend we're having a normal conversation," said Addie placidly. "But someone in the audience is watching us."

I kept my eyes on the show, fighting my immediate inclination to look around. "Yeah?"

"He looks familiar," said Addie, still talking like we were discussing the weather. "I think I've seen him before. In New York, I mean. That's how I first noticed him. So I pretended to leave so I could watch him from another vantage point. He kept looking toward us every few seconds, like a nervous tic. I don't know who he is . . . but I *definitely* recognize him."

"Where is he?" asked Kira. I was impressed with her subtlety—there'd been a time when she'd already've given us away.

"Don't look," Addie warned. "He's back three rows and to the right. Blue button-up shirt and a Bieber cut. Any idea what this could be about?"

"Mob guy, I bet," said Kira. "Should I scare him?"

"Please don't," said Addie. "It would probab—"

"Hey, keep it down!" whispered a woman behind us. "Some of us are trying to watch a show!"

Addie clamped her lips together . . . for all of ten seconds before continuing her rebuttal, this time several decibels softer. "Hostile action toward a mobster. Not a good idea."

"Bullshit. He's stalking us. That's hostile. He did it first." Somehow, Kira managed to match—and not wildly escalate—Addie's volume.

I held up a hand for silence. Normally, I'd have let the discussion flow around me while I considered, but we'd already been called on our volume once, and I didn't wanna draw more attention to our conversation. Addie and Kira obediently stopped talking and waited for me to weigh the pros and cons of our various options. Finally, I had my verdict.

"Let him be for now," I whispered. "Addie, keep an eye out and tell me next time you see him. I want more info before we do anything. But if he—"

A loud cheer erupted around us and Addie jumped, startled. I turned my attention back toward the stage. Magic Miles'd just removed his pants, revealing a golden half-thong. My brain tried to figure out how it stayed on before I forced it away from that vein of thought and back to more productive—and less disturbing—matters.

"If he's fucking with us, his ties to the mob won't save him," I finished.

Kira grinned, satisfied, and Addie squeezed my arm appreciatively. I'm pretty sure both of them thought I was secretly on their side and conceding to the other to keep peace within the group. I saw no reason to dispel that perception.

I spent the show's last few minutes thinking about our watcher. Kira'd called him a mobster, and we'd gone with that hypothesis, but we didn't have any evidence for it. Then again, who else could it be? I ran through my list of enemies, but none of them seemed likely. It could *maybe* be the man we were here to find, but I dismissed that hypothesis on the grounds that it made absolutely no sense.

One thing was certain, though—I wasn't just gonna leave him alone too much longer. Plans work best when you minimize the variables, and the presence of an unknown man keeping tabs on us for unknown reasons had the potential to be a game-changing factor. Letting him alone would be an amateur mistake.

Miles took his bows to thunderous applause, and then the curtain swept closed in front of him. The crowd began filing out of the theater, drawn by the promise of other flashy diversions. Addie reached under her seat and retrieved a bouquet of yellow and blue flowers.

The actor's entrance to the backstage was guarded, but it was hardly Fort Knox. All getting past security took was waving the flowers, saying we were here to see Miles Dutch (knowing his full name legitimized us somehow, even if it *was* publicly available to anyone who'd done their research) and continuing through the door before the guard could mention we looked a little young to be hanging around a casino.

Miles was (thankfully) already dressed by the time we found his dressing room. The half-thong lay discarded on a nearby chair, while the rest of his gaudy magician's outfit was heaped in a corner.

"Hello, Miles," I said, holding out a hand. Miles instinctively turned toward us. His brow furrowed in confusion, but before he could ask who we were, Addie was pressing the flowers into his hand.

"Great job!" she bubbled, sounding exactly like an overzealous fangirl. I had to stifle a snort remembering how dismissive she'd been of his act just minutes ago.

"Hi," I said quickly, using the opening she'd created. "We're friends of Z's. He told us to check out your act."

The furrows in Miles' brow grew deeper. "Z?"

Oh, right.

"Um . . . metro black guy, afro about yea big that he's super into, a little shorter than me? C'mon, he said you guys were friends."

Comprehension dawned. "Oh! Zare."

"Yeah, him. We just, uh . . . we call him Z for short."

"How is he?" Miles asked enthusiastically. "Is he here?"

"No, he couldn't make it," said Addie, sighing dramatically. "He really missed out."

"Yeah, it was awesome," I said. "But he was actually hoping you could help us. It's not a big deal—we just wanna know if you've ever seen this man." I pulled the blurry picture up and passed him my phone.

I wasn't exactly holding my breath. There was no way a randomly selected entertainer in a Las Vegas casino would happen to know a Mafia-affiliated man who wasn't even necessarily *in* Las Vegas. But we had to start somewhere, and maybe Miles would say something like *no, sorry, but here's who might . . .*

Miles lifted one eyebrow. "Is this a joke?" he asked. His voice was soft, but expressive—entirely different from the showman's voice he'd been affecting onstage. For some reason, it made me think of warm honey spreading slowly across a table.

"Um . . . no?"

"Well, of *course* I know him," said Miles, still looking mildly confused.

*What?* My jaw tried to drop, but I'd already clamped my mouth shut in anticipation of its treachery, so all I did was grimace weirdly. What were the odds of *that*?

"But if Zare knew I'd know, why didn't he just tell you?"

"Maybe he just wanted us to see your show," I said quickly, stopping Miles' train of thought before it could start arriving at dangerous conclusions. "But since we've come this far, you might as well tell us."

"Well," Miles smiled winningly, a hint of the showman creeping back into his bearing. "Anything for a fan. He's our head of security. Why'd you wanna know?"

# FIVE

"I'M APPROACHING THE FRONT ENTRANCE," SAID Addie softly in my ear. "Preparing to arrive. Stay positioned. Where are you situated?"

I peeked around the slot machine in front of me, doing my best to avoid looking at the prominent *Jorgensen Financial Consulting* ad on the far wall, which featured a color portrait of Lucas's smug face blown up to three times its normal size. "I'm in the main front gambling area. My machine's . . . six rows back from the front door, at the very end of the row, on the side farthest from the entrance, on the left."

There was a short pause. Then Kira, who was also on the line, said, "Got it."

I leaned back in my chair, fed another fiver into the machine, and pulled the lever. A few seconds later, I was out five dollars. "Awww, man," I said grumpily, and reached into my pocket for another bill. I was, in short, the very model of a modern addict gambler. Guys like that were ten to the penny here, and they were too focused on their slots to even *think* about participating in a casino heist. My goal was to give off the same impression

We'd spent three days after getting the tip-off from Miles planning, prepping, and researching. Sounds like a lot, but we'd spent barely half our self-allotted time, and we were pretty much *done*. If everything went smoothly, we'd finish on day four and spend the rest of our vacation on the Revel.

First things first, the man in the picture—Paul Ford, or so Miles'd identified him. Some Google wizardry confirmed Miles's intel—his full name, headshot, and place of employment popped up the moment we started typing. From there, the plan would practically write itself.

But just *having* a plan didn't make us ready. We needed a few key pieces. Kira'd had to track down some specialized software, Addie'd had to stalk some New York, New York employees and indulge in a little petty burglary, and I'd been stuck on my laptop, researching the exact parameters, specs, and legalities of the casino's impressive stable of slot machines.

And all our preparation culminated in Addie walking through New York, New York's entrance plaza dressed in a worker's uniform, carrying two flash drives in her breast pocket and a keypad combination in her head.

"I see you," she said. "Don't turn your head."

I hadn't been about to.

"Shut up." That was Kira. "Folks'll think you're talking to yourself."

The earpiece fell silent.

The wallet twisted in my fingers as I had a faux-crisis of indecision about placing another bet. Finally, my self-destructive side "won" and I slid another bill into the machine. This time, there was a celebratory bell, accompanied by a soft whirr as the machine spat out a small ticket with the words CASHOUT VOUCHER above the amount it was worth at the counter—fifteen dollars. Not bad.

*"Alright, you can talk, sheesh. You're worrying me. Where are you?"*

After about thirty seconds of tense silence, Addie replied. "Sorry—had to find a free place to talk. I'm in, the code worked. I'm almost at the main computer nest."

"Cool. You remember what you gotta do?"

"No," said Addie sarcastically. "We only went over it a dozen times or so—"

"A-ight, listen close. You find an open computer and plug in the drive that looks like a little dog. Then—"

"I was kidding."

"Oh. Right, I knew that."

"Okay," said Addie. "I'm going in. That

means I can't talk to you guys anymore. Wish me luck . . . "

"Good luck, babe," I said, trying to make it look like I was talking to the slot machine.

In my head, I pictured the scene—Addie, using her worker's uniform as camouflage, creeping through the room of overworked and oblivious IT professionals to an unoccupied workstation, sitting down like it was her own, and sticking the first flash drive into the slot.

If Kira's word was reliable—and when it came to computers, it usually was—the first flash drive contained something she'd called a brute-force algorithm. Basically, if it was plugged into a computer that required a password to unlock, the program entered randomly generated strings until something worked. It was capable of trying millions of potential passwords per second. A common encryption—like most personal computer passwords—wouldn't last longer than thirty seconds.

With popular security features, the account

locked down if you gave more than three wrong passwords. Kira claimed the device could bypass that too, and when I'd asked her how it worked, about half the terms she'd used went over my head, so I'd nodded and pretended I understood.

I heard nothing over my connection for a while until Kira said, "Eight-nine-two-two-one. 'Kay, I'm in."

The second flash drive, which Addie would've plugged in after the first got her past the password screen, actually *was* a data storage device and not a hacker's tool. This one contained a program Kira'd downloaded earlier today. If you ran the software on two computers simultaneously, you could remotely access one using the other's hardware. Once Addie had the program running, all she had to do was input the number Kira gave her and Kira'd have complete control.

"Um, this is my workstation, buddy," said Addie suddenly, aggressively.

Crap. I'd hoped this wouldn't happen, but you

can only make so many plans that rely on people staying absent before someone finally *doesn't*.

"Sleep the screen," said Kira immediately.

"You got the wrong station," said Addie. "I've been here all day. What, me? How can you not know me? We've been working together for years!"

"Stay cool," said Kira, and I couldn't tell which of us she was talking to. "I'm working on it. I still have access through my monitor. They've got some fun security measures in here, but nothing the Kirameister can't handle."

There were rustling noises coming through the headset now, sounds of a commotion I couldn't identify. My heart hammered in my throat as I pictured Addie tackled to the ground by overzealous casino security. And all I could do was sit back and pull this lever.

"Alright, let's talk to the big guy," said Addie. "He'll tell you I'm right."

"Thanks," said Kira. "Appreciate it."

New York, New York had invested tens of

millions of dollars into new, improved slot machine technology. You could tell the machines themselves were new by their glossy back frames, and their lack of stains and gaudy plastic. There were some retro machines deeper in for the nostalgia-afflicted gambler, but near the front, all the old models'd been retired and replaced with the latest in gambling hardware.

The selling point of the new WMS-made slots was the lack of reliance on internal machinery. The slots were interlinked through a central computer system that regulated each slot's payout and kept the system as a whole taking in more than it paid out. You could monitor machine popularity over time, extrapolate blocks of data from a big enough sample, and keep automated logs of every system to ensure protection against tampering.

More importantly, with the right security clearance (or Kira's skills), you could manually set the odds of a spin paying out, machine by machine.

A sudden outburst of shouting came through

over the headset. Serious shouting, it sounded like—but as Addie wasn't making the noise, it was difficult to tell.

"The hell's going on?" I asked over Kira asking the same question—only with a barrage of expletives.

"Improvising," Addie grunted. She was breathing heavily. "Kira, hurry."

Clicking boots on the tile. My head twitched toward the sound to see seven navy blue-uniformed, radio-sporting, gun-toting men with crew cuts and dour expressions walking swiftly past my row. They were drawing eyes all around the gambling area—this apparently didn't happen every day.

"Seven boots en route, maybe more," I said, hiding my mouth behind my hand as I faked a cough.

There was a loud, crackly sigh. "Figured. Heat's off me for now, but I need a better hiding place. And a way out. Jason, any bright ideas?"

"Sneak out during the diversion? That's too easy."

If I'd needed to come up with a diversion on the spot, it might've been a challenge. But we had one ready-made, already built into the plan's framework. Addie couldn't have asked for a better opportunity.

"Got it," said Kira triumphantly. "Told you bitches. Jason, you're up. You get my drives?"

"Grabbed them before I skipped." Addie's voice was more smug than it currently had a right to be. "I don't forget things like that."

I was too busy feeding twenties into my machine to participate in the conversation. One after another they vanished, like cookies into a hungry child's mouth. The "play count" in the corner of the machine ticked higher and higher.

"Fack," said Kira. "I can't raise the jackpot higher than five-point-four-two percent."

"Well, raise it that high and log off before someone turns on that computer," I snapped. Seriously, you introduce one small wrinkle into the plan and *everyone* goes off their game. Why's it always *my* job to make sure things don't fall to shit? Not being able to crank the odds up to one hundred percent *would* significantly impact the expected value of my winnings—but it didn't matter *too* much, in the context of the plan.

"Done," said Kira abruptly. "You have your super-machine. Disabling cameras in three . . . two . . ."

My right hand rested on the lever, itching with anticipation.

"One . . . you're good."

I started pulling the lever as fast as I could, blowing through my available plays.

At the same moment, the fire alarms went off.

And chaos swept New York, New York.

Patrons looked around, shocked and confused. Some ran for the exit, some ran toward the nearest staffer, some ran to find their friends or family . . . but just about *everyone* ran. Staff tried to cope, likely receiving orders on the fly, but the mass of people they needed to herd was too large and too sudden. It was a vast, uncontrollable mob—kinda like the streets of the real New York City.

And in the middle of it all, one teenage genius, calmly pulling his lever and removing tickets from the machine as fast as it could spit them out.

Roughly once every twenty spins, the machine lit up and made a big spectacle. Nobody noticed.

There was a buzzing in my ear, but I couldn't make it out over the general noise. Hopefully nothing important, but I didn't wanna risk it—I needed a place I could talk to my partners in crime. There was no reason to stay, as my plays were now at zero and the machine'd stopped vomiting tickets. They were in my wallet, my pockets, my waistband—anywhere they'd fit. It was a windfall, a fortune . . . provided I took my winnings to the counter for exchange. Which might raise questions.

No, I'd keep the tickets for now.

Someone tapped my shoulder. I spun around prepared for the worst, already formulating a lie.

"Time to go," said Kira. "This party's about to head downhill."

Not trusting my voice to carry over the noise like hers could, I made a thumbs-up and stood to follow her, ignoring the sensation of innumerable slot vouchers digging into my belly.

Having Kira with me made getting to the exit incredibly easy. She just shoved, elbowed, or (in one case) head-butted her way through anyone who blocked our path. I tagged behind her, making sure nobody was taking an interest in us. I sincerely doubted, though, that casino security'd be occupied with the slot floor. For all they knew, a full-on robbery could be taking place, *Ocean's Eleven*-style. There were higher-priority areas to defend.

When we were a few hundred yards from New York, New York, I opened my phone to find a text from Addie.

made it 2 the crowd & they lost me. where r u?

Relief swept over me. If she'd made it that far, she was as good as safe. Addie in a crowd might as well've been the wind—invisible, uncatchable.

Safe outside. Come join us when you feel like it.

I grinned at Kira. "She's safe."

Then I started pulling tickets out of my pants. "Can you take some of these? They're getting uncomfortable."

# SIX

THE VERY NEXT DAY, WE WERE BACK AT THE SCENE of the crime—which any criminal worth the title knows is a bad idea. But once an idea gets bad enough, people stop suspecting it. Nobody could *possibly* be dumb enough to rob a casino and then walk right into the head of security's office . . . right?

"Here's one in the *Times*," said Kira, waving her smartphone under my nose. "*Slot Machine Targeted In Casino Heist.* Oh, this one's boring."

Word of our exploits had spread like a salacious rumor through the various news outlets, and we'd been amusing ourselves reading them to each other, assigning points for accuracy. Reuters was currently in the lead with one hundred thirty-seven points, but said points were assigned with all the care of your average *Whose Line* episode, so the real front-runner was anyone's guess.

"BuzzFeed has a list of *Twenty-three Signs Your Casino Security Needs Improvement*," Kira tried. "Number one. You—"

"No BuzzFeed please," said Addie. "I get enough of that shit on my wall."

"No BuzzFeed?"

"Clickbait crap," I agreed. "Let it die."

Addie gave me a high-five, which somehow turned into us holding hands. This whole relationship thing was *nice*.

"Oh, c'mon," said Kira. "It's so funny! They know my life!"

Addie gave Kira her best frosty glare, which I'm well acquainted with. It's the one that means she isn't actually mad—when she *is*, she hides it much better. Her *best* glare's reserved for when she's play-acting anger. It's a subtle distinction. Slowly but steadily, I was becoming more and more of an expert on the enigma that was Addie, though that secret behind her eyes, the one that first intrigued me, remained hidden.

Someday.

"Like they *invade* my life," I said. "They were on my stream so much, I had to start sorting people into different circles based on how often they spammed me."

Both Addie and Kira slowly turned and regarded me like I was a scientific curiosity.

"You know, your stream. Like a Facebook feed, but in Google plus."

They were still giving me that odd look. "What?"

Addie sighed. "Jason, nobody uses Google plus."

The resulting argument over which social network was superior lasted until the concierge we were waiting for returned, and ended inconclusively.

"Mr. Ford's waiting in his office," she said, with palpable venom dripping through her sugar-sweet smile. She'd kept us waiting almost twenty minutes, and honestly, I couldn't blame her given what we'd put her and her coworkers through. Today, Addie was pretending to be an *incredibly* anal-retentive New York, New York stockholder who was afraid yesterday's security failure would ruin her investment. With pure bluster and fire, she'd arranged a meeting on short notice with Paul Ford himself to secure his utmost assurances. It'd taken almost a full hour of arguing, and by the time Addie'd gotten her way, she'd been on her third concierge and I'd resolved to stay on her good side by any means necessary. As the concierge opened Ford's office door and waved us in, I saw her cast a sympathetic look over our heads.

Mr. Ford waved us into his cramped office with a resigned motion, looking down at his computer screen. He seemed altogether too large for the room, shoulders bent, lurking like a tiger in the mist. Every bit as imposing as the day we'd met in Van Buren High's parking lot.

But with the mystery stripped from him, much of the effect was gone. Now he was Paul Ford, white-collar worker. And he was in big trouble with everyone who mattered. There was no more mystique about him. And I'd left Van Buren High forever.

Addie cleared her throat and Mr. Ford glanced up.

Our eyes met. And not in a romantic way.

There was a soft *click* as Kira shut the door behind us.

"We're here to help you," I said quickly as he reached for the desk's phone. He froze, unconvinced, and Addie sauntered over to the desk and shut his computer. He stared open-mouthed at her, still flabbergasted by our appearance in his office.

"Hear us out," she said. "I promise, you'll want to listen to this."

Mr. Ford retracted his hand, responding to some subtle undertone of honesty. I tried to stifle my envy, not quite successfully. What I wouldn't give to be that persuasive.

"Mr. Paul Ford," she continued. "I take it from your reaction that you recognize us, so I won't bother with introductions. We're here about the heist."

"How'd you find me?" asked Mr. Ford, ignoring Addie's spiel.

Addie, not to be deterred, ignored him right back. "When I posed as a disgruntled investor, I was lying. But your staff's reaction tells me you've seen a few real ones already. You're being hounded from all sides, Mr. Ford. Investors, media, your boss, coworkers seeking your position—you were sitting in the big chair when this heist occurred, so you're the one they've marked to dump their blame. I'll bet you've been dealing with inquiries all day."

He nodded tiredly. "I suppose I shouldn't expect answers from you kids. Alright. Yes, I am. And because of that, I am a very busy man, so if you're here to help me, you'd better start."

It was right about now that I realized Mr. Ford didn't have a place for guests to sit. I thought about mentioning how rude this was, but didn't wanna interrupt Addie while she was doing her thing, so I leaned against the wall, trying to make it look like I was doing it to look cool and not because my legs were starting to complain. There hadn't been a place to sit while we were waiting, either. Was this what passed for customer service these days?

"First," said Addie, "I would like to fully establish your position. You're looking at a modest severance package and a termination of your employment. You'll probably have to find work in a different sector entirely, given the public blowback of this disaster. It'll be a black mark on your record to anyone with an internet connection and your full name. Seems a bit of a shame to me . . . so I figured we could help you do something about it."

Mr. Ford brightened at that. Now we were not only offering him something he needed, we were speaking a language he understood. "How much?"

"Oh, not much of anything, really," said Addie. She tapped her foot against the floor absentmindedly. "Just one name."

As accommodating as Mr. Ford had become at Addie's previous remark, that one shut him down cold. His body language shifted into outright hostility and his lips narrowed. "*Now* I understand."

"I see you do," said Addie, matching his shift with a more dominant stance. "I wasn't expecting you to be eager about it, *Mr. Big*. But surely you need all the help you can get? Or is your job worth nothing to you?"

Mr. Ford sat like a marble statue behind his desk. His eyes flicked about the room, lighting on each of us one by one. If he noticed we numbered three instead of four, he didn't mention it.

"And if you're doubting how much help we can be, you should know—*we* pulled yesterday's heist," said Addie. "We have over sixty-seven million dollars in cashout vouchers. Now, we *could* distribute them through the city's population in a slow trickle, allowing them to be redeemed a few at a time. Or, we could give them back. Every last one."

Ah, the endless one-two punch of carrot and stick. How effective it was, even if you were anticipating it.

"That's how you save your job, Paul—by returning the vouchers yourself. Claim it was a training exercise—one the security team failed. You present them with the plan we used, outline why it succeeded, and present your proposal for preventing them in the future. You come out aggressive, like you have nothing to be ashamed of, and the world will eat it up. And like magic, all your negative PR spins positive. All we need is one simple name."

"I didn't know his name," Mr. Ford rumbled, looking down at his desk.

Addie leaned down to his level, slapping her hands against the desktop. "Excuse me?"

He lifted his head to meet her eyes. "I don't know his name."

Addie frowned, disappointed. "So you don't."

This wasn't exactly unexpected. In the criminal underworld—much like in bad fantasy literature—names can be powerful things. You could work with a team for years and never learn your colleagues' real identities. It was safer that way, for the express reason that it prevented people from doing exactly what we were currently attempting.

"Alright then," said Addie. "My offer's negotiable. In absence of a name, the story will do. The *full* story."

She waited for him to start talking. Then, when it became obvious he wouldn't, she prompted him. "You can start by explaining why a famous casino's head of security flew across the country to hire four high schoolers for the Mafia."

Paul Ford pursed his lips and exhaled, like he was blowing away the last shreds of his resolve. "You'll return the money and disappear?"

"You have my word," said Addie, and Kira and I nodded our support.

"Well, then." He pursed his lips again, this time

in thought. "Alright, let me explain. This job pays nowhere near enough. Not for a house in Las Vegas, anyway. I make it up on the side. Unofficially, I'm a liaison." He paused. "A liaison's someone who—"

"We know what a liaison is, old man," I said. Addie shot me a look, and she was right to do so, but I'll be damned if I let a man twice my age talk down to me like I'm an amateur. Though anecdotal evidence suggests I'd be just as annoyed no matter how much older he was. Or younger. Arrogance just pisses me off in general. There's not enough space in the room for *my* ego as it is.

"My apologies. Well, I do a fairly robust business with the local families. They give me the jobs, I find the people. You meet the most talented crooks as a head of security, and all of them need some kind of way out. Especially once you've caught them."

Mr. Ford chuckled and opened the center drawer. Kira tensed and stepped forward, but the object he pulled out was nothing but a fat cigar. "Mind if I smoke?"

Addie shook her head. "Go ahead."

"Where was I? Right. The Mafia." Mr. Ford lit his cigar and puffed pensively. "The Bonannos wanted this basketball game rigged, so they dropped me a notice. I was asked to find them a team. That's when *he* got in contact with me" (emphasis being mine, because it certainly felt ominous at the time, but now that I think about it, there was nothing odd about how he said "he").

"Like I said, I never got his name. Used a burner phone, too. When he hung up, I had no way to contact him. But he said he knew what the Mafia'd asked me to do. He said he had just the people in mind for the job, that it was imperative they do it. Paid me some serious money, plus expenses. Gave me your contact info and sent me to New York to rope you in by any means necessary. Money, favors, threats—whatever." He gulped. "That's all I know. I did my job. The game was rigged. I got paid. Figured that was it."

I looked at Kira and Addie, conferring with them

silently. If Mr. Ford was telling the truth, we had a fat load of nothing to go on. We'd expected to find the man behind the plot, but we'd come up against another link in the chain.

I could tell Addie was thinking the same. "That's very helpful, thank you," she lied. "Is there really *nothing* else you can tell us? It's very important. Remember, as soon as we think we have enough, we'll return the jackpot receipts."

Mr. Ford kneaded his forehead with his fists and pursed his lips yet again, obviously thinking hard. "Right. Yeah, I got something. The guy I talked to was insistent—no parents. I couldn't let the parents suspect a thing. That's what stood out at the time. It was weird. Like, why would parents be involved? But when I heard how old you all were, it made sense."

"And you only spoke to him the once?"

"That's right. I didn't have a way to call him back, and he never called a second time. Found the cash in my account a little later, and stopped thinking about it. Never thought I'd see you kids again." He chuckled. "Good work. Really, how did you find me?"

"Friend of a friend," said Addie carefully. "Now, the money. Did—"

"Tell me about the phone's security," Kira blurted.

Addie was far too professional to chide a colleague in front of an outsider, but I could tell it was taking just about *all* her self-control.

"Uh, you know," Kira continued awkwardly, noticing Addie's disapproval. "Did he block caller ID, or what?"

"Yeah, he blocked it," said Mr. Ford tiredly. "I called in a favor at the comm office and got the number, but it'd already been disabled. Tried tracing it, no luck. That's when I gave up. What more can you do?"

"*Now* we're getting somewhere," said Addie. "So you got the number. What was its area code?"

Mr. Ford looked uncomfortable. "That's not

reliable info—area codes are real easy to fake if you know what you're—"

"And many people don't. What was the code?"

"Two-oh-two. Washington, DC, I looked it up first thing."

The last puzzle piece fell into place, which was weird, because they'd been nothing but a jumbled mess before now. Imagine the odds of a small tornado dropping down, sweeping up a pile of puzzle pieces, then dropping them to the ground locked together as one complete puzzle. Paul Ford's answer was that tornado.

"That's it," I said, slapping the nearest surface—a modest bookshelf with a convenient hand's worth of empty space. "I've got a theory. No, a hypothesis. At the very least, a lead to follow up on."

It was all based on an assumption I was making— that whoever wanted us to take that job didn't have our best interests in mind. The fact that the mob had tried to bump us off afterward had always struck me as odd, but it made much more sense if someone'd asked—no, *paid*—them to. This line of thought'd always ended with a problem—why not just pay them to kill us without adding the job? The Mafia was happy to do contract killings, for the right price.

But if you were trying to throw an investigation off your trail, it made sense. Detectives would get as far as "they worked for the Mafia, then were quietly killed instead of paid" and declare the case closed.

Now I had a motive. That narrowed the search field down to people who wanted us dead—a larger field than you might guess. But add a DC area code to the mix, and pray that *meant* something and hadn't been picked at random to further muddy the waters, well . . . it could only be one person.

And as simple as that, our faceless enemy had a face.

# SEVEN

**R**ICHARD TRIEZE. OUR FIRST BIG TARGET.

He'd tried to have us killed once, and the attempt'd cost him two million dollars. When you lose that big, there are only two ways you can react. You can take the hint and walk away at a loss, or you can double down.

"You have my word that if you don't fuck with me or mine, I'll let you be." I'd said those exact words to him on the New York City docks, facing down the barrels of him and his favorite henchman, Thomas. At the time, he'd seemed scared enough to take my warning to heart. Had something changed?

The moment I shared my hypothesis with Kira and Addie—that being as soon as we'd left the casino—they instantly agreed. That threw me a little, since I'm used to my friends trashing my plans before I prove how ingenious they are. In fact, having no opposition from the peanut gallery very nearly got me to reconsider everything I was thinking until I came to my senses and realized that every so often a broken clock told the right time.

We'd had the rest of the week to consider the implications of Richard Trieze's potential sudden reappearance in our lives. Kira'd been the first to decide that if my hypothesis was correct, Richard was indirectly responsible for every bad thing that'd happened to us. He'd sent us to Vegas, which had led to our feud with the Mafia, which had led to . . .

It'd be a load off my mind if the blame for *that* debacle rested at Richard's curiously tiny feet.

"That *dicktree*," Kira'd cursed. The nickname stuck.

If—and again, I must qualify the statement—*if* Richard was responsible, he'd forfeited any right to protection under the truce we'd made on Pier Eleven. And while our last attempt at revenge-plotting hadn't ended well, this was different. We weren't up against an entrenched criminal organization—just one man. One we'd beaten soundly more than once before.

I'd seen his true face—what was left once his jokes and giggles fell away. He was menacing. Cold-voiced and blazing-eyed, like a malevolent spirit—exactly the kind of person you'd expect to find high on the corporate ladder. Yes, he was certainly capable of setting us up to die. Heartless enough to target teenagers, cowardly enough to do it through a third party—a class act. Clearly, Richard didn't score too highly in the "moral fiber" category. Kinda like a certain hedge fund manager I knew.

"Alright, what do we have on him?" Addie asked. "I remember we researched his background for the poker game job, what was that?"

We were having a preemptive "war meeting" to discuss possible courses of action against our former mark—a meeting that Kira'd promptly volunteered to get drinks for, then never returned. I suspect it was a silent protest of our decision to spend precious hours of our last day in Vegas talking in our hotel. And she had a point, but Addie'd been adamant, and I could hardly side *against* her when she was being level-headed and responsible. Oh well, Kira tended to stay quiet during the planning meetings anyway—it was *on* the job that she became insufferable.

I opened up the relevant docs. "Let's see . . . Oh man, look at this pic. I forgot how ugly he was. Yeah, look, we've got loads of info, down to his blood type—B positive, by the way. He's thirty-four, or was when I gathered all this stuff . . . "

Addie leaned down and rested her chin on my shoulder, reading faster than I could dictate.

"*Damn*," she said. "He's rich."

"Yeah, he's got money," I said. Approximately thirty million, to be exact—plus his gains since I'd assembled the dossier. The two million I'd demanded to buy his safety would've barely inconvenienced him. It was just enough that he'd remember us long after we'd parted ways . . . and not fondly.

"Imperial Tech?" she asked, noting his place of employment.

I opened a new window. "Yeah, I Wiki-ed it last time I compiled this. It's a pretty successful software company. Richard built it from the ground up fresh out of Tufts."

"He's an impressive guy," Addie noted.

"Not where it matters," I said. Too late, I realized that could be interpreted all sorts of ways, and not just *we beat him pretty easily last time*.

Addie laughed. "Easy for you to say."

"I meant . . . oh, forget it."

Addie snaked her arms around me, still balancing her head on my shoulder. "Don't worry. I'm not going to leave you for Richard Trieze. Now relax a bit, alright?"

*Relax* . . . I tried, but I had no idea what I was doing. I tried slouching a little, but it didn't feel right. I hadn't relaxed in years—did my body even remember how?

"You're so tense," said Addie, withdrawing. I opened my mouth to object, but her hands were on my back, kneading at it tenderly. "Would it kill you to take it easy occasionally?"

"You sound like Kira," I protested, closing my eyes and letting her hands work what magic they could through my shirt.

"Maybe you should listen to her more often," said Addie. "Sure, I wouldn't want her in charge, but the girl knows how stay loose. Better than we do, anyway."

"But then I wouldn't be so tense, and you wouldn't be giving me this massage."

Addie made an exasperated noise and swatted at the back of my head.

"You figured out what's up with her yet?" I asked suddenly. "What she was lying about, anything like that?"

I'd been ignoring Kira's issues for too long. Addie and I'd talked about it a few times since Z left the group, always when we were sure we were alone and wouldn't be overheard. But—as we *were* sure we were alone—these talks never lasted too long before we found ourselves sidetracked by more enjoyable pastimes.

Addie was silent for a bit before she replied. "Let's talk about that later," she said quietly, as one of us eventually did every time the subject was raised. Never before, though, had it happened *that* quickly.

"Just, Kira isn't here right now," Addie

explained. "Do we have to drag her back into the mix? I'd rather be alone with you."

It was hard to argue with that logic when my girlfriend's hands were moving across my back, playing xylophone with my shoulder muscles. After all, we could always discuss Kira later . . .

Addie's lips touched the back of my neck. The ghost of the kiss lingered a few seconds after they left. I leaned back, tilted my head upward, and met her mouth with mine. She responded enthusiastically, hungrily, foregoing all pretext of a massage. Then—

A loud, mocking cough from the doorway.

Addie and I froze mid-kiss, then simultaneously turned to glare daggers at Kira, who was standing in the door with the *biggest* smirk on her face.

"Fucking shit," she said, tossing a twelve-pack of something I'd bet everything I owned was root beer onto the bed. "I leave you kids alone fifteen minutes and you're already going at it. You'd never get anything done if I wasn't here to break you apart."

"No, we were working," I said in my best *who, me?* voice. "You just walked in at a bad time."

"I'll say," chuckled Kira. "Next time, I'll make *you* get the root beer. Then the ladies can concentrate on the job instead of practicing for the Makeout Olympics. Unless . . . "

Kira wiggled her eyebrows at Addie suggestively.

"I prefer my partners *without* root beer breath," said Addie coolly. "And Kira, disregard my drink order again, and I'll get your family audited. I asked for Fanta. As usual. And you got me root beer. As usual."

"Yeah, 'cause you fucked up and accidentally didn't order the best kind. As usual."

"Forget it," said Addie, shaking her head with disgust. "Next time, *I* get the drinks."

"And leave me to make out with *that one*?" said Kira in a voice so laden with horror, I'd consider it an insult if I didn't know exactly where she was coming from. We're like oil and water, sexually speaking. Cerebrally, I know her combination of looks and danger lust is practically magnetic to some people—to the point that in sophomore year, some people had a betting pool going where the first person to make out with her won the pot. When *that* reached the CPC's ears through the grapevine, I entered the pool and "won" . . . and we promptly mutually agreed to never let something like that happen again. Not even for half a two-hundred-seventy-two-dollar pot.

Addie shook her head again. "There's no binary choice between getting drinks and kissing someone. That's a fallacy. The false dilemma."

"*You're* a fallacy," Kira shot back.

"I . . . don't even know how to respond to that."

"That means I win."

"But—"

"No more arguing. I already won."

Addie rolled her eyes.

"Forget it," she said. "I'm going back to being

productive. Which we *were* doing while you were out."

She tapped the spacebar to brighten the dimmed screen and pointed to the Imperial Tech Wikipedia page I'd opened. "See?"

"Yup," said Kira, joining her behind the chair. "One open webpage you haven't started scrolling down yet. Hard at work."

My snappy retort died on my tongue as I actually *read* the page I'd opened.

There, near the bottom of the opening paragraph, was a short, innocuous sentence—*In March 2015, Imperial Tech was acquired by Jorgensen International for $20 million.*

Kira and Addie continued their friendly bickering, but I tuned them out. *Jorgensen International. There* was a name not worth the breath it took to say it. And not a name I'd expected to see on Imperial Tech's Wikipedia page.

For some reason, Lucas'd been interested in Richard's company. And March 2015 put the date of the buyout right around the time we'd rigged the poker game.

"Guys," I said. Then, a little louder, "*Guys*. I think this is important."

The argument stopped.

I pointed at the screen, where it said *Jorgensen International.* Addie's eyes narrowed when she saw it. Like me, she was thinking through all the different things this could mean.

"That's Lucas's company," I said for Kira's benefit.

Kira frowned. "Who's—oh, right, your dad."

"Yes, my . . . yes."

"He didn't want any parents getting involved," said Addie slowly. "Or maybe, one parent in particular. The one with the power over his job."

I was already pulling up another window, looking for more information about the purchase. Soon, I had what I needed—a more exact date. Jorgensen International'd bought Imperial Tech just over a week after the incident at the docks.

These things just don't happen by coincidence.

"Makes sense," said Kira. "If I was going after my boss's son, I'd wanna keep it secret too."

I put another tally mark in the "Richard's behind everything" column of my mental scorecard. "I'd say from this point forward, we're operating under the assumption that it *was* Mr. Dicktree."

This raised the question of why Lucas would buy out Imperial Tech. The answer came easily enough—he knows something of my interaction with Richard. Which meant the question was actually, how much does he know? And what did buying the company accomplish?

But there, my train of thought ended. I simply didn't have enough information to make reasonable guesses about the situation.

Guess I'd just have to find some.

"Anyone up for another vacation?" I asked.

Kira grinned. "DC?"

"DC."

Addie raised her hand. "Point of order. Here,

we were fish out of water without Z. We were lucky—"

"—And I was smart—"

"—But that may not be the case in DC. I don't want to go in blind again. And if there's any chance we're going after the guy who got us involved with the Mafia . . . "

Her voice trailed off, but I could tell where her train of thought led. She didn't want to say it. None of us did.

"It's only fair to give him the same chance," I said at last. "That's what you think."

Addie was silent, but I read agreement on her face.

I never could deny those eyes.

"Well, call him up," I said. "I'll let him say no to you himself."

# EIGHT

*CLICK.*

The link I'd clicked behaved exactly as a link should—which hadn't necessarily been a guarantee. Kira'd created this web page from scratch, and my job was to test it for bugs before she hacked a major company's website and uploaded her creation in its place. In the corner, Addie was practicing her "generic polite announcement" voice.

"If I'd known it'd take this much work to rope Z into the job, I'd have just said no," I muttered, clicking a few more random spots.

"If Z weren't such a jerkass, it wouldn't have taken this much work," said Addie, still sounding for all the world like a telemarketer who'd gotten enough experience to nail the voice, but hadn't been working long enough to lose her zesty spark.

"Maybe we should've taken the hint when he ignored the first round of calls," I said, but I knew that at that point, it'd become more about us than about Z. He'd given us a *challenge*.

And had we ever risen to it.

Kira's room hadn't lost its chaotic ambiance since the last time we'd used it as an impromptu base of operations . . . as we do *every* time we need an impromptu base of operations. You'd think we'd be used to the clutter by now—it ebbs and flows, but never quite reaches "acceptable".

"Everything looks good," I said to Kira, who was hovering over me. "I didn't make anything break, anyway."

"I ripped most of it from their source code," said Kira. "*That* stuff was always gonna work. It's the rest I was having trouble with. Get up."

I did, and Kira slid herself back into the chair.

"Thanks for warming it for me," she said. "We're ready to go live on your okay. Hopefully it takes them a while to revert the changes."

I glanced at Addie, and she indicated her readiness with a minute nod. Asking her was just a formality, really—she'd been ready hours ago. She didn't really *need* all this practice, but she practiced anyway, just in case. Went beyond what was expected of her to make sure it was done *right*.

Just one more reason why Addie's awesome.

Kira stuffed a pair of earbuds into her ears, and her fingers started tapping the keyboard in an arrhythmic beat. Tinny death metal blared from her general area, and from the look on her face, Addie could hear it too.

Sometimes I worry about Kira's hearing. Then I realize she doesn't listen to me half the time as it is. *Then* I wonder if her disobedient streak comes from being unable to hear my orders.

Come to think of it, what if Kira's current

dynamic within the group was based on a series of implausible but hilarious misunderstandings?

Nah.

"We're live," said Kira smugly. "Abalone Smooth has a new home page until their underpaid CS interns realize there's a problem."

"Turn it off or I'm not putting him on speaker," Addie threatened, gesturing at the earbuds. She'd eventually ceded to our demands to put the phone in speaker mode on the condition that we make absolutely *no* noise, not even giggles. Naturally, Kira and I had consented immediately.

Kira gave Addie the stink-eye, but complied, stuffing the iPod back into her purse. As soon as everything was quiet, Addie dialed Z's number.

She was using the burner app, of course. Just because Richard hadn't been tech-savvy enough to avoid buying a whole other phone didn't mean *we* had to limit ourselves.

The time between rings felt longer than normal, stretched out. I'm not sure why, but I was holding my breath as I counted. One ring . . . two . . . three . . .

And then it stopped, and we were on the line with Z for the first time in months.

Addie cleared her throat. "Hello. Am I speaking to Mr. . . . Zelgius Davis?"

Her voice was precisely metered, candy-coated, and *nothing* like her usual voice. No way could Z recognize it through the veneer of fakeness she'd plastered it with.

"Who is this?" Z's voice came in loud and clear through the speaker. He sounded just the same as he always had.

Hearing it stirred up old memories, and I suddenly couldn't believe the club'd been limping along without him. The four of us were a team. We needed each other.

"This is Ms. Dorothy Trilling, with Abalone Smooth Fine Hair Care Products, hoping to speak with a Mr. Zelgius Davis," said Addie with a touch of insistence.

Z didn't respond right away, and for a moment I thought he'd picked up on the ruse. Thankfully, my fears turned out to be groundless. "Yeah, this is him—I mean, me. So, uh . . . how can I help you?"

"Congratulations," said Addie cheerily. "You've been selected to win the grand prize in our recent sweepstakes! An all-expenses-paid trip to . . . " She trailed off, realizing he'd hung up. "Crap. I should've been less spammy."

She re-dialed. This time, Z picked up on the first ring. "Hello?"

"Mr. Zelgius Davis?"

"Oh, hell."

"Mr. Davis, I promise you this is not a scam," said Addie quickly, before he decided to hang up again. "I understand your skepticism, but Abalone Smooth has a long history of giving back to its loyal customers. This call is entirely on the level."

"Oh," said Z, still sounding suspicious. "Sorry, I guess."

"As I was saying, you've been selected to win

the grand prize in our recent sweepstakes! An all-expenses-paid—"

"I didn't enter any sweepstakes."

"All that was necessary to qualify was a purchase of at least one Abalone Smooth Fine Hair Care Products item between the months of January and May," said Addie without stumbling. With Z's passion for his hair, it was all but guaranteed he'd bought something within that time frame. "The details are on our website."

"Huh," said Z. Addie waited a few seconds for more, but that was all he said.

"You're our grand prize winner, which means an all-expenses-paid trip to Washington, DC, and a date with a mystery movie star!" she said, filling the awkward silence with pure enthusiasm. "You'll be picked up from your house by limousine and taken right to the famous five-star restaurant, Marcel's, where your date will be waiting. After dinner, the limo will take you two on a tour of the Smithsonian museums, famous landmarks and monuments, and all our nation's capital has to offer. Later, you'll be asked to try our newest brand of conditioner and provide feedback directly to Abalone Smooth's president. Again," she stressed, "this is all explained in detail on our website."

"Well, it sounds . . . holy shit," said Z, and Addie laughed a horrid, fake little laugh. "Who's the date?" he asked.

"It's a surprise!" Addie burbled, winking at Kira. I almost snorted with laughter and gave the entire thing away, but I managed to keep my composure by imagining what Addie'd do to me (or, more likely, *not* do to me) if I laughed. "The mystery is part of the experience, but trust us when we guarantee you won't be disappointed."

Of all the lies Addie'd told this conversation, that one was probably the biggest.

"When's the trip?" asked Z.

"The relevant information is available through our website, www-dot-abalone-advantage-dot-com," said Addie. We'd arranged the vacation to be in five days, which Addie was well aware of, but it was important that Z check the website *now*, while Kira's handiwork was still up. If he checked later and found no mention of the sweepstakes, he'd know for sure that something fishy was going on. As if reading my mind, Addie continued. "Please be aware, now that we have selected a winner, we will not have information on the sweepstakes prominently displayed too much longer. If you need to contact us with any questions during this time period, please email customer support at abalone-advantage-dot-com, or call our helpline directly at one-eight-hundred-two-two-one-four-four-six-oh."

"Got it," replied Z, accompanied by the sound of rapid typing. I looked at Kira questioningly and she gave me a thumbs-up from behind the screen—the fake page was still up, containing all the bogus but official-looking information Z could ever want.

And just in case he went looking for that customer support email, Kira'd gotten into the "contact us" page and changed some things there too—but *these* changes were harder to catch. We were proud owners of the domain *abaioneadvantage.com*, which contained a functional email client. Naturally, we'd registered the email *support@abaioneadvantage.com*, and Kira had listed it as Abalone Smooth's official contact email—only she'd capitalized the "i", which meant that short of running tests (which Z had no reason to do) or having particularly sharp eyes (which Z didn't), there was no way to distinguish the previous *support@abaloneadvantage.com* listing from the current *support@abaIoneadvantage.com*. Only difference was, if Z clicked it and tried to send a message, it'd arrive in our inbox instead of theirs.

And the phone number? Abalone Smooth's website didn't have one listed. So either Z'd remember the number Addie'd just given him and call it (reaching the phone line we'd prepared for that circumstance), use his phone history to re-dial Addie (in which case, great) or go looking for the number on the website, fail to find it, and use email instead (which, as I've established, we controlled).

"Alright," said Z after about a minute of silent research. "Looks like I'm all set."

"Great," beamed Addie. "Our limousine will pick you up at one in the afternoon on Friday. Thank you for using Abalone Smooth Fine Hair Care Products! Stay clean!"

"Yeah, you too," said Z. "Bye, Ms. Trilling."

"Goodbye." *Click.*

Addie tucked the phone into her pocket and waited for us to congratulate her, but we both said nothing at all.

"For the love of—I hung up," said Addie, rolling her eyes and throwing one of Kira's innumerable stuffed toys in our general direction. "You guys can talk now."

"*Stay clean?*" I asked, raising an eyebrow. I'm a sucker for dramatic irony, but referencing the CPC like that was probably pushing it a little. Z's not dumb—for that matter, he's smarter than he lets on. After Addie'd tried calling him and discovered he'd blocked our numbers, I'd vetoed trying alternate methods of communication because I'd known that if we made too much of an effort at the onset, he'd be on the lookout for a trick like this.

In fact, if I were him, I'd check with a friend of mine at Abalone Smooth. Someone I trusted, just to make sure everything was legit. That'd be the cautious thing to do . . . *if* Z were as paranoid as me. If he weren't so eager to believe he was getting a once-in-a-lifetime chance to meet a movie star.

There's something called the Litany of Tarski, which is a short, easy-to-remember phrase. "If something's true, I want to believe it's true. If something *isn't* true, I *don't* want to believe it's true." Seems simple enough in theory, but you'd be surprised how hard it is for people to live that principle in their day-to-day lives. There're whole industries, both legal and otherwise, that reap their profits by telling their marks what they *want to believe*. And if a statement holds that most privileged position in your mind, you're not gonna try too hard to disprove it.

This was the weakness in the human mind I was counting on—that Z's *desire* for this date to be real overrode his bullshit detector. He *did* like his starlets, after all . . .

Addie smirked. "I couldn't help myself. You would've done it too, don't lie."

"Guilty as charged," I said. "But that doesn't mean I won't blame you if he figures it out."

"You think that's a possibility?"

"Z's a dumbass about this shit," said Kira. "He's gonna spend the next few days wondering which celeb he gets to try and hook up with."

"Try not to disappoint him *too* much," I ribbed, and Kira slugged me lightly on the arm.

"You're lucky I agreed to this," she said. "I'm only in it for the limo ride."

I exchanged glances with Addie, and we could see agreement in each other's eyes. *Don't tell her she doesn't get to ride in the limousine until it's already too late.*

**NINE**

"I *STILL* CAN'T BELIEVE I DIDN'T GET TO RIDE IN THE limo," Kira sulked.

"If you had, he would've seen you before he got here," Addie said for the fifth time. "The point is to keep him in the dark until he's already here. In no way does your taking the limo further that goal."

Kira exhaled forcefully and started balling up her napkin.

Marcel's was my kind of restaurant. Calming, understated decor, religiously attentive waitstaff, and prices high enough to keep out the riffraff. You couldn't even just order an appetizer and soak up the ambiance because Marcel's was a *table d'hôte*—the *prix fixe* started at ninety dollars for a four-course meal and only climbed from there. It was *exactly* the sort of place you wanna win an all-expenses-paid trip to, and the sort of place we couldn't have afforded if I hadn't dipped into my personal savings . . . *again.*

It was also the sort of place that didn't tolerate bad manners. I tapped the table and caught Kira's eye—we'd *discussed* this. One by one, her fingers peeled away from the napkin, letting it fall back into her lap. Luckily, it didn't look like anyone'd noticed.

Now that her right hand was unoccupied, Kira reached into the basket at the center of the table for another piece of bread.

"Don't get crumbs on your dress," said Addie automatically. Kira was wearing an absolute stunner of a dress—strapless, in iridescent blue that deepened into a dark purple near the floor, with a maroon sash around the waist. Below the sash, the dress flared outward in waves, like her legs'd been enveloped in a large blue-purple cloud. She really *did* look like a movie star out on a date, especially with her hair down and strategically combed to cover the raised flesh that formed the scar on her left cheek.

She'd definitely gone the most all-out. I'd picked classic black-tie attire, but then, there aren't exactly myriad options when it comes to men's fancy dress. Addie, too, had gone with basic black, bias-cut. She looked great in it—I'd told her as much, and gotten a, "Cool," for my troubles.

I've always been at home in suits, and Addie can make just about any fashion work for her, but Kira was looking decidedly uncomfortable and out of place in her red carpet-pilfered masterpiece, so naturally, Addie and I were reminding her what she was wearing whenever we got the chance.

"Great choice, by the way," I remarked as Kira stuck a cube of butter onto her bread without spreading it, then bit the whole thing in half. "I like how the blonde flows into the blue, and then into the purple. It's a nice effect."

"Shuddub," said Kira through her mouthful of bread. Which, as anyone who's eaten enough meals with Kira will know, translated to "shut up."

I found Addie's foot under the table and winked at her. She smiled back, but glanced pointedly at her phone, which was lying next to her plate. I checked my own and noted, with a wrinkle of disappointment, that it was five fifty-seven.

"We *did* tell the driver to arrive at six exactly," said Addie. "So as much as I'd like to . . . "

"Like to what?" asked Kira suspiciously.

"Keep gazing at that beautiful dress of yours," I tried.

"Never mind," said Addie quickly as Kira made neck-wringing hand motions at me. "Point is, we should go to Places. For the sake of review, that's Kira artfully posed against the big stone vase by the front door, Jason documenting Z's reaction for later entertainment, and me observing and reporting from outside, on standby in case something needs doing."

Kira pushed back her chair and stood. "Got it," she said. "My prince better not keep me waiting."

She'd been much happier thinking of the plan as a massive prank on Z than as a date. Go figure.

I took my position by the door, partially obscured by a hanging curtain, and pulled out my trusty Galaxy S6. I didn't wanna miss a single second of this. I was gonna preserve the footage forever and watch it in my old age whenever I was feeling nostalgic.

We'd scraped the bottom of our dwindling finances to make the setup as grandiose as we could—we even had a camera crew waiting outside to ambush Z as he left the limo, ostensibly to document the date. The head of the crew had orders to indicate to Z that his team was there to get some star shots . . . which would hopefully get Z speculating on his date's identity all over again. And then he'd walk through the gate and into the restaurant (we'd wanted to lay down an actual red carpet and line it with paparazzi, but we hadn't had the funds, and besides, restaurant staff might've objected) and see Kira, dressed better than he'd have ever seen her, posing coyly, probably shaking with laughter, and me, immortalizing the whole scene on video.

*This* was artistry. *This* was the spirit of the CPC—that surrealistic moment when a good prank comes to fruition and the world turns upside-down for one poor soul.

"I see the limo," said Addie's voice in my ear, and I had to stop myself from breaking out into giggles, which would've been *incredibly* embarrassing given the company I was in. I wasn't worried about Z spotting Addie and putting two and two together—nothing and nobody can spot Addie if she doesn't wanna be seen. You get in the habit of occasionally saying, "Hi, Addie" when you're alone in a room, just to check if she's there. One time, she even responded.

"Pulling up . . . he's out. Crew's going wild," Addie reported with glee. "Z's got this beautiful smirk on his face, the kind that would be tempting fate if this were a movie. They're taking some shots for the tabloids."

I made a mental note to myself to buy those pictures and save them for a rainy day.

There was a murmur rising in the general area. Put a camera crew in front of a limo, and people're gonna notice. They were talking, speculating, updating their social media profiles. There was something big going on—or so they thought.

If I could do it over again, I'd probably change the plan so it attracted less public attention. Who knows which of the parasitic twenty-four-hour-news networks would decide this disturbance was worth mentioning, and who could be in the right place at the right time to see it. In our profession, visibility of any kind's almost never optimal.

"He's headed for the door."

I readjusted my phone one last time, then

hit *play*. A few seconds later, the restaurant door opened and Z, my one-time friend and associate, stepped through it.

He was looking far more put together than I ever remembered seeing him, in a slimming, navy blue, three-piece suit that looked fresh off the iron. His dark hair—as always—shone with a healthy, no doubt nutrient-bath-assisted, glow. There was a confident swagger in the way he held himself, a tilt to his pelvis, shoulders open wide.

He was set to make the most of his evening, impress his date as much as possible, and—possibly, it *was* Z, after all—turn the night into a profitable venture. And it *showed*.

And then his eyes lighted on Kira, still standing innocently against the stone vase, and his composure vanished like it'd never existed.

She gave him the tiniest of waves and winked. (I couldn't see her face, but I know Kira, and I'd bet every penny I've ever owned that she had.)

If you can imagine the total collapse of an

empire but on a smaller scale, you can imagine Z's face when he and Kira locked eyes. It was almost tragic—but not tragic enough for me to stop filming.

He was stunned. Floored. The disappointment lingered on his face for *at least* eight seconds before it started draining away into resentment and smoldering anger as he put everything together. Then he wheeled around and threw Marcel's door open again.

Addie chose this moment to make her appearance, heading off his exit. I wasn't close enough to hear her normally, but my earpiece had no problem picking up the slack. "We didn't go to all this trouble so you could turn around and leave."

She put a hand on his shoulder—a pacifying hand, but a forceful one nonetheless. He tried to shrug it off and push past her, but she held firm.

"The limo's gone. You're stuck without a ride, and that's one pricey taxi. So you can—"

Z cut her off with a few words I couldn't hear.

I started edging closer, hoping I could catch both sides of the conversation.

"Or hear us out, and don't stand your date up," said Addie. Her eyes twitched toward me as I approached. Though her face gave nothing away, that momentary glance was enough for Z to notice and he turned around—though thankfully slowly enough that I could hastily jam my phone back in my pocket.

There was a long, tense pause.

"Of *course*," scowled Z. "Crew's not complete without Jason Jorgensen."

"Naturally . . . excepting the sarcastic tone," I said, giving Z my best friendly smile. "Not without you either, dude. How've you been?"

He didn't even crack a smile. "What do you want?"

Behind him, Addie gave me a look that said, "You're not helping." I ignored her.

"We're playing the revenge game again. The right way, this time."

"Figures," Z snorted. "Didn't learn your lesson the first time. Course, it wasn't *your* dad that died."

"Look—"

"But you would've been fine with that, right?" Z's glare practically skewered me against the wall. This wasn't how I'd pictured this conversation going at all.

And it was taking everything I had to refrain from pointing out that it'd been *Hector's* idea to go upstairs, not mine. That'd end any chance we had of getting Z back. Though it went against my every instinct, I had to take it on the chin until he'd gotten blaming me out of his system.

"What's the holdup?" said Kira, who'd finally decided to join us. "I'm fucking hungry. Let's sit back down."

"Forget it," snapped Z. "I should've known this was a setup. I'm out."

"And pay a fortune in cab fare?" I asked skeptically. The Z I knew was more frugal than *that*.

Z gave me a superior look. "*That's* what y'all

were relying on? I've got friends in DC. One of them'll probably gimme a ride home."

I hadn't thought of that.

"It's a *very big favor* to ask," said Z, grinding the words between his teeth. "And I'm *not happy* about having to ask it. I can't believe this. I had shit to *do* today, and y'all thought you'd pull me a few hours outta my way to ask me back on your *team*. Like we're still *friends*. Y'all wanted me to be impressed? Well, it's a massive fucking inconvenience, is what it is."

"Pretty funny though," said Kira. "You should've seen your face."

Z turned on her, opened his mouth, caught himself, and swallowed. Addie took a surreptitious step closer to me and nudged me softly.

"It *was* a little funny, I guess," muttered Z. "From an outside point of view."

I shook my head despairingly. If Z's crush on Kira ended up saving this plan, it might've been better off failing.

Kira smiled broadly. "Right? You're a funny guy, you can enjoy the humor of the situation. Like, you get news you've won a random prize! That's never legit. But then you start thinking it is. And then you find out—surprise!—it was bogus all along. That's more than just a dastardly scheme, that's *art*."

Z sighed. "See, that's what I don't get. Y'all want me to help you, so you hassle me and then try to make me laugh at how hassled I am. That ain't—"

"Not seeing the problem," Kira interrupted, grabbing Z's hand and yanking him toward the dining area through a pair of waiters who'd been trying to determine if they should intervene in our argument or not. "Just chat with us, 'kay? You're already here, and dinner's on us."

Addie and I followed, exchanging amused glances. But I wasn't sure this was a good idea in the long term. I had no idea if Kira knew about Z's crush, and none of us really wanted to tell her.

"I *am* already here," I heard Z concede, giving ground reluctantly before Kira's persistence. "Revenge, huh?"

"Allow me to explain," I said, catching up to them with quick strides. "We found the guy who—"

I stopped, stumbled over my words as Z looked at me.

There was a coldness in his eyes deeper than his otherwise passive expression. Coldness, and hatred too. And I was reminded that right now, Z was looking at the person he saw as responsible for his father's death. And only the possibility that there was someone else he could blame was keeping him here right now.

That stare was a warning, unintentional or no. *Kira may be talking me into this despite my better judgment, but you are not forgiven.*

But he'd noticed my sudden stammer, and his brow was wrinkling in confusion, so I recovered before he could wonder *why*.

"It's Richard Trieze—the guy who kidnapped you."

I realized as I said it that, given Z's track record, that only *somewhat* narrowed it down. But he nodded once, curtly. He recognized the name.

"We, ah, we're putting together a plan," I said, lowering my voice another notch. It didn't hurt to be careful. "But we need an in with a local crime organization. Not the Mafia. And, well . . . if the last few months taught us anything, it's that we need you."

It was an attempt at reconciliation—but judging by Z's response, a poor one. He didn't react at all, not even a blink to hint that he was any closer to forgiving me for my greatest failure.

"I know a guy or two," he said. "Tell me the rest and I'll think about it over dinner."

He grabbed some bread out of the newly-replenished bread basket. "And no matter what I decide, you're giving me a ride back."

# TEN

"Isn't the Triad more of a West Coast thing?" Addie asked.

"Every big-time criminal group has people in DC," said Z. "Folks whose job it is to stay legitimate, make sure Congress ain't passing anything that'll hurt them too much. Lobbyists, working night and day to keep the gangs safe from the biggest group of crooks in the country."

He gave a not-so-subtle look in the direction of the Capitol building.

Z's sour mood'd abated somewhat since last night, though he was still cold toward me. I'd pretty much given up on changing that, at least in the near future—there's only so much processing power I can devote to solving problems, and our revenge on Richard Trieze was currently more pressing.

I could handle Z being mad at me, as long as he did his job.

And to be fair, he totally had. Fewer than twelve hours after we'd filled him in, he'd gotten us a meeting with the heads of the local Triad chapter. We were waiting on a street corner for his contact, who'd be leading us to the meeting location. The Triad were apparently sticklers for security.

But then, if *I* were the ranking representative of a multinational criminal enterprise in the same city as a national government, I'd take every precaution as well . . .

"Jesus *dicks* I'm hungry," Kira complained. "Can we get something to eat?"

"Not without the risk of missing our contact," I said. "She's due any minute."

"I've been starving since last night." she groused.

"That place had the *smallest* portions. If you're charging me that much per plate, I at least wanna be filled up. Know what I'm saying? What a rip-off."

I bristled. "Marcel's is a five-star dining experience. You're not supposed to gorge yourself like a pig. You dress up nice—"

"Yeah, and thank baby Jesus that's over," said Kira. "I couldn't *move* in that dress."

"You looked good," said Z.

Addie and I exchanged significant glances.

Kira shrugged. "I felt lousy."

Z must've caught our glances out of the corner of his eye because he backpedaled almost immediately. "Like, it was just so unexpected. Seeing y'all was bad enough, and then it was like, whoa. Kira's in a *dress.* And that's how I knew things were serious, because otherwise you never would've put something like that on."

My phone buzzed—a text. And from Addie, to my surprise. But she must've had a reason for texting me from five feet away (it was probably a quip regarding Z's crush), so I didn't even look her way as I opened it.

watcher frm vegas apprx 60ft back.

My blood ran cold. *Someone* wanted to keep an eye on us. And I was pretty sure I knew who it was.

I started texting Kira. Treaty with the Mafia or not, I was *not* gonna tolerate some goon of Lorenzo's following me around wherever I went. I'd played nice long enough—it was time to send a message.

Kira looked at her phone and then immediately up at me. "Why'd you—*oh*." Addie just rolled her eyes at Kira's lack of subtlety.

we doing this? Kira asked telephonically.

We're doing this.

"I think we passed it," I said loudly. "What street was it again?"

"Fuck if I remember," said Kira.

I wheeled around. "C'mon."

It was *impossible* to resist sneaking a glance at our tail as I started back up the sidewalk—I hadn't seen him yet, after all. He was sallow-skinned and bespectacled, with a scraggly dark beard. Naturally, he kept walking toward us after we'd turned. Had to stay innocuous.

As we passed, Kira grabbed him firmly by the upper arm.

He pulled. Kira planted her feet and didn't give an inch.

He kicked. Kira danced nimbly out of the way and swept his legs out from under him, sending him tumbling to the concrete.

"Z," I said. "Can you make sure nobody's interested in intervening?"

For once, he didn't offer any objections, but moved off obediently.

I looked around warily. We were *completely* exposed. We could play on the sympathies of law enforcement if they showed up—he *had* been stalking us—but our contact could always get spooked and duck out if this became too big a scene. *I* certainly would in his position.

Kira was dragging the man to his feet again, albeit a little worse for wear.

"We saw you in New York," I said, trying not to let my misgivings show. "And again in Vegas. Now here, tailing us. I don't need you to admit it—it's *obvious*. It's less obvious what'll become of you. My first thought's to hand you to the police, but there's room to make a deal. Let's start with your employer's name."

I hadn't expected a reply, and didn't get one. I shrugged. "Your choice."

Addie began to dial slowly. Nine . . . one . . . one . . . and then, after one last pause, *talk*.

"Nine-one-one. What's your emergency?"

The man's expression didn't so much as flicker and Addie hung up.

"Not scared of the law, then," I said. "Are they in the Mafia's pocket here too?"

Out of the corner of my eye, I allowed myself a

look at Z as he chatted amiably with a concerned-looking pedestrian. He was doing his best, but there was only one of him. He couldn't be *everywhere.*

"Over there," I jerked my head toward an alleyway and Kira's grip on his arms strengthened. He twisted again, trying to wriggle free, but her hold was implacable, and he became resigned to his fate once that failed.

While dragging someone into an alley's shady as fuck, at least this way Z could cover half the entry points at once. Given pedestrian volume, that'd *hopefully* be enough—it wasn't a weekend, so the tourists weren't out in force.

As soon as we were situated behind a small dumpster with Z posted by the nearest alleyway entrance, I turned to Kira and said, dispassionately, "Break his fingers."

*That* got to him in a way my previous threat hadn't, but he still said nothing as Kira wrenched his arm up by the wrist and grabbed hold of his pinkie.

"Cover his mouth," I said to Addie, and she reached a slim hand toward his face. He pulled his head away. When she made another attempt, he started thrashing madly.

And yet he didn't call for help.

Kira tightened her grip and, smiling grimly, kept bending his pinkie back.

"Your employer," I demanded as his face distorted in pain.

"Fine," he squeezed out at last. Feeling a surge of triumph, I signaled Kira to stop.

"I'll talk!" he growled, a little louder. Addie jabbed Kira in the ribs and she let go, looking almost disappointed. The man slumped, breathing hard and cradling his hand. He wouldn't meet my eye.

"Tell me," I said. "Or she starts again."

It was a bluff this time. I wasn't gonna trust Kira with pretending to break someone's fingers if I couldn't fucking trust her to *stop*. I'd thought

I had her *figured out.* Wasn't she supposed to be trying to leave this shit behind?

"Lucas Jorgensen," he said at last. "Your father."

It was such an unexpected answer, I didn't even register what I'd heard for several seconds.

And then the bombshell hit.

Lucas *knew everything.*

No. No, that wasn't necessarily true. He knew *some* of it, certainly. And I wouldn't put it past him to've assigned me tails since I first left the house. But it wasn't a *given* —

"How long has he had me followed?"

And then came the *second* bombshell as I remembered—Jorgensen International'd *bought Imperial Tech.*

Shortly after, Richard'd concocted a plan to have us killed.

And now that we were avenging ourselves on Richard, Lucas was having us *shadowed.*

With a coldness in the pit of my stomach, I

allowed for the possibility that Lucas Jorgensen was moving against me.

"Xander Davis?"

Broken out of my reverie, I looked toward the alleyway entrance. In front of Z stood a young Chinese woman.

I noticed that in the time it'd taken her to speak, Addie'd managed to slip behind a nearby lamppost.

"That's me," said Z.

She looked past him, at the four of us only partially hidden by the dumpster, frozen in a tableau. "Let him go."

"But—"

"You are attracting undue attention. Let him go, or you will not make your rendezvous."

I weighed the two options, one against the other. Revenge against intel. But in the end, we had an Op to finish. Distractions could be pursued later.

"Fine," I spat, and Kira released her captive's

arms. "But if we see you following us again, we'll kill you. And that goes for all of Lucas's pet spies."

He scuttled down the alley in the other direction, turned the corner sharply, and vanished.

A little time to digest that encounter would've been nice, but I didn't have that luxury—I had a Triad representative to deal with. She was a little taller than Addie, slender, with dyed blonde hair and a confident stance. As she and Z walked toward us, I noticed she held several long strips of fabric.

"Sorry about that," I said. "Personal business."

She raised one eyebrow—just like I've always *wished* I could do. "More important than your meeting with Wo Hop To?"

I didn't say what I was thinking, which was *possibly*. In fact, I tried to put anything related to *Lucas's* involvement in all this out of my head entirely . . . for the moment.

Instead, I said "It was a momentary distraction, and I apologize."

This, she seemed to accept. "Then follow,

without further delay," she said. "My car is parked nearby. I will ask you to blindfold yourselves once you are inside. The Dragon Head does not wish for visitors to know his location."

"Fair enough," said Z, taking a strip of cloth and motioning us to do the same. We did. When her hands were empty, the woman beckoned us to follow her.

"Xander?" Kira muttered to Z as we walked. "Like, with an *X*? You're slipping, dude."

"It sounds the same, and there's only so many names," said Z. "So shut up."

We reached the car, a black Nissan with extended rear seating. Our mysterious courier opened the rear doors for us, then watched us fumble with our blindfolds. I obediently tied the thick fabric around my head as prompted . . . not mentioning that I'd surreptitiously set my iPhone to update my location every two minutes on a private, friendless Facebook profile I'd created for this exact eventuality.

The cloth fit snugly over my eyes, letting in small gaps of light at the edges. Seconds after I finished, I felt small fingers tugging at the blindfold, centering it, making sure it was properly placed. The gaps of light disappeared. Then a light touch on my back guided me toward the car.

I wondered idly what someone passing by would think, then decided most of them weren't even noticing us. Humans're pretty good at discarding information they perceive as extraneous to their current situation, regardless of how odd it gets. It's a phenomenon known as *selective attention,* and the most well-known psychological experiment highlighting the effect is Harvard University's infamous "Gorilla video".

Participants were asked to watch a short video in which two teams were passing around two different basketballs, and count how many times one team passed. Upon reaching the end, they'd have an answer . . . but have missed the gorilla that'd wandered into the center of the shot in the process. To over half the participants, the gorilla was effectively invisible—and so, I hoped, were we.

Remembering the gorilla experiment helped me focus on something *other* than the possible machinations of Lucas Jorgensen, but it wasn't quite enough to block out his mocking laughter.

The front seat was quiet for the entirety of the short journey, and the rear seats weren't much louder. There just wasn't much any of us felt like saying in the presence of a gangster, even if she *wasn't* currently planning on killing us.

As far as I knew. Of course, if she *were*, blindfolding us under the pretense of paranoia was a good first step. Realizing this wasn't exactly *calming*, and memories of the *last* time a member of a criminal syndicate'd driven us somewhere didn't help matters.

After a short-but-not-insignificant length of time, the car stopped moving and didn't start again. Next thing I knew, my door opened and our driver was asking us to get out and hold hands.

She grabbed my left hand to start and, after a few tentative grabs with my right, I found a hand I immediately recognized as Addie's. I gave it a squeeze and she squeezed back. Then her middle finger started tapping against my knuckle in an even rhythm.

I counted twenty-six taps before she stopped. The drive, according to Addie's count, had been almost a half-hour long. I filed this information away for later—you never know what'll suddenly become relevant when you need a plan.

"Watch your step," our guide warned softly, and I lifted my feet high over the lip of an open door. She gave several more navigational instructions as we continued through whatever building we'd entered. I inhaled deeply often, trying to pick up whatever smells I could. There was one section where I smelled new paint, and another where I smelled a burning candle, but the place seemed pretty odorless besides that.

Then, just up a long flight of stairs, a sharp,

smoky smell of citrus. Incense, maybe? My personal bet was on incense.

It was to the center of that pungent room that we were led, and then a sharp left. The guide's hand slipped out of my own. "Drop your hands," she commanded.

I reluctantly parted ways with Addie.

Something pressed against my lower legs.

"Sit," said the Chinese woman. I reached behind me just to confirm the thing I was feeling was, in fact, a chair. There seemed to be a surface where I expected one to be, so I sat.

"You are in the presence of the local Dragon Head of Wo Hop To," said the guide. "Through the good word of Jiang Chongan, you have been granted audience. You have leave to speak."

Finally. I reached up to drop my blindfold . . . and received a sharp blow to the stomach from an unknown source. I coughed, more from surprise than pain, and withdrew my hands.

"Your blindfolds will remain on, so that you

may not identify the Dragon Head in the future," our guide explained dispassionately. "He will look upon you, but you will not look upon him. Further attempts to gainsay his measures will be punished more harshly."

I cleared my throat—the room's vapors weren't being kind to it. "I'm sorry. Ah . . . Mr. Dragon Head, thank you for taking the time to meet with us. We're here to beg a favor, one which hides an opportunity for mutual gain."

After Z'd pointed out that the Triad was a patriarchal organization, we'd decided as a group that I'd negotiate rather than Addie, even if she *was* the best negotiator we had. She was waiting silently to correct me if I put my foot in my mouth, and Z was ready to talk if our personal connection to the Triad was questioned. Kira, on the other hand, had been cautioned to stay quiet at all costs.

Silence from the room. I continued. "It's come to my attention that among its other activities, Wo Hop To hosts infrequent underground gambling events . . . I would ask that we be allowed to organize and run the next."

Someone spoke a flurry of deep-voiced Chinese and our guide translated. "Why do you ask this?"

Honesty. Honesty first. "There's a man in this city who's wronged us. He has a great weakness for gambling—I expect he's frequented your tables and will again. Through this game, we'll put him in debt to Wo Hop To, and thus gain power over him. Wo Hop To will be handsomely paid, and we will have our revenge."

*"Jason,"* hissed Addie, softer than a breath.

The man who'd spoken before was laughing mockingly. Again, our guide hastened to translate as he spoke. "There is no sum of money worth Wo Hop To's honor, fool. Our organization is not a tool to be used by a group of children still adding sums in school."

"This is to our mutual benefit," I explained quickly. "You are no tool, but a partner. If you're worried about honor, you could blame the unfortunate affair on us. Wo Hop To could claim that a false game was organized in its name, using resources cleverly faked or stolen, impossibly authentic but entirely unsanctioned. In truth, we don't have the resources to do such a thing, which is why we've come to you. But if you were to say such a thing had happened, and that it never would again, why, no gambler in Washington would hold it against you . . . "

My voice trailed off, and into the silence was spoken a single word which I'd already translated before our guide did it for me. "No."

"I urge you to fully consider the opportunity presented—"

"Young man, you and your milk-fed companions begin to test my patience. I am not blessed with infinite time that I may waste it on fools."

I forced my breathing to stay even. We *needed* the Triad's cooperation—maybe there was a time we wouldn't have, once, but right now we didn't have the money to pull this off ourselves. That last refusal'd sounded pretty final, but there had to be a way to turn this around as long as I stayed calm and the others didn't—

"You're a bunch of fucking idiots," said Kira.

My blood turned to ice in my veins. I'd *warned* her—

"Jason's giving you a risk-free way to make some serious cash, and you're—"

"*Kira*," said Addie with a voice full of warning.

"—Blowing it off like it's no big deal. Well, if you limp-dick assholes knew what kinda cash we were talking about here, you'd—"

There was an awful, shudder-inducing *smacking* noise and Kira's tirade was cut off abruptly. I turned in her direction, *willing* myself to see past my blindfold and perceive what'd happened to her, but of course, it didn't work and I decided trying to take off the blindfold again would be a Very Bad Idea. I noticed I was breathing quickly and tried to shut that down. I needed to be calm.

Needed to somehow spin this into a win. Needed to . . .

"Members of Wo Hop To's family learn a simple lesson that you apparently lack," said the guide, voice devoid of any inflection the original Chinese sentences'd possessed. "To not speak until you have made peace with the consequences of your words."

Another loud smack and a grunt from Kira. And then a long stretch of silence where I didn't trust my voice to speak.

The Dragon Head began again. "I will not lie, I am impressed," said the guide. "To take not one, but two blows from Liang without undue expression of pain is a feat I am ill acquainted with."

"Didn't even feel it," said Kira.

I sent a silent prayer of thanks to any gods that might be listening that Kira'd somehow managed to keep her volatile temper through being smacked twice, and hadn't retaliated—either verbally or physically.

"It is more than I expected of children," said the Dragon Head through our guide. "I respect those who accept their lessons without complaint, and learn them in the process. It is a skill my own family does not always possess. Have you learned your lesson, girl?"

If Kira didn't say yes, I'd strangle her with my bare hands, even if it cost me my life. Or set her up on a blind date with Z.

"Oh, yeah," said Kira. "Yeah. I get it."

"Good," said the Dragon Head in perfect English. "Then let us drop the pretenses and talk in detail about this proposal of yours. Perhaps I will find it to my liking."

# ELEVEN

WE HAD OUR GAME.

Poker again, just like we knew Richard liked it. High stakes, just like we knew he liked to play. Rigged as hell, just like he hated.

This should be intuitive, but it's so much easier to rig a game *against* someone than to game the odds in one person's favor. Barely an hour into the night and poor Richard was already down thirty Gs. Even with the eighty percent cut the Triad'd "negotiated" out of us (paid under the table, of course—the Dragon Head'd been clear that if evidence implicating the Triad was ever uncovered, we wouldn't have heads to look over our shoulders for the rest of our lives with), we stood to gain a great deal of money.

*A great deal of money*—one of my favorite phrases, that. Too long had the CPC been in a financial rut, practically reduced to turning up its metaphorical couch cushions for loose change. After tonight, if all went according to plan—and it *would*, there was no reason it wouldn't—the gang would have its groove back.

As Richard lost hand after hand, my big regret was that I couldn't be there in person to watch. It was simply too risky. Even if I'd had an excuse for my presence, my face was probably forever associated in Richard's mind with rigged poker games, and that association could lead him down paths of thought we'd rather stayed closed.

(Not that associating us with rigged poker games was *unfair*, mind you—just unfortunate.)

But we couldn't just *not be there*, or there'd be nobody to work the plan. So Addie'd thrown together yet another brilliant disguise and was currently managing the counter as Hsiao Xiuying (which'd rolled off her tongue like she was a native speaker, much to our awe).

"My Chinese isn't so good," Addie'd said when briefing us on her chosen character. "I'll probably be American-born, so I have an excuse for being more comfortable with English."

"Isn't so good?" I'd said, bewildered. "You mean you know it?"

"Not as well as I should," she'd replied, to which I'd pointed out that one could only be expected to know so many languages, and that she deserved a little slack given how many she already had in her back pocket. But that hadn't stopped her from buying an advanced book on learning Chinese and insisting she'd be at its teaching level by September.

A real overachiever, my girlfriend.

She was looking stunning, as always, in a bright green cocktail dress, wearing her chin-length black hair in a bob. The last time we'd rigged a poker game, she'd cut it short to better fit inside a wig, but it was slowly growing back.

Kira, like me and Z, lacked the ability to lose herself in a character and become unrecognizable. But she was needed onsite, so she'd curled up behind the counter in an alcove—which'd been built for storing booze and *not* Kira-sized humans. Her computer balanced precariously on her stomach and her mouth was covered by a strip of black tape, mostly as a reminder.

That left myself and Z, who, lacking both a purpose and a safe place to be, were one floor up, watching the proceedings on the room's security feed. Kira'd rigged it earlier so we got sound near the counter, which was the important place. So we watched and listened, let the ladies do the dirty work, and tried not to acknowledge the other's presence too much. I'd said, "Hello," when he'd come in, and he'd given me a jerky nod. And I mean *jerky* in both senses. That dick.

Richard threw down his cards in disgust and

one of his tablemates claimed the haphazard pile of bills and chips in the center. He stood up from the table, said something neither of us could hear, and stormed over to the counter where Addie was working. It was hard to tell over the cameras, but I was sure Richard was in one of his *moods*—he wasn't good at keeping calm if things weren't going his way. Thanks to the rest of the table (and a handy bit of game theory), they weren't.

It was always tense when Richard stepped up to the counter. Not only was every interaction between him and Addie another opportunity for him to recognize her, I worried each time that he was about to cut his losses and cash out. My worry was unfounded, though—he didn't have it in him to do something that sensible.

"Ten more, please," he said to Addie, voice clear through the strategically placed mics.

"Yes, sir," said Addie smoothly. "The protocols are the same."

"Of course," said Richard, and handed Addie a credit card.

Addie eyed it as she swiped it through the reader. "On your third already?"

To this, Richard made no reply.

In any competitive business, those who survive are those who best adapt to emergent technology, and it was our good fortune that the Triad'd taken so amicably to modern ways of money-management. While some old-fashioned venues limited their clientele to paper, the Triad had an entire money-laundering framework in place to allow those in need of extra cash to withdraw whatever they needed, right there at the game.

Of course, this meant trusting a criminal organization with personal information, which is why the Triad was adamant about protecting their trustworthiness. Maintaining their spotless record was a better long-term financial (and legal) decision than committing identity theft. Surprisingly, their focus on providing a safe environment had *worked*, and now all but the most paranoid put their financial security in the Triad's hands during their games.

But if an unassociated group was able to ape the *appearance* of a Triad-sponsored game, well . . . *they* had no incentive to make good long-term decisions, did they?

On the monitor, Richard returned to the game with an additional ten thousand dollars in chips, and the game began again.

The game was a drama, an illusion played out for the few people at the table who weren't in on the secret. Those were the regulars, people Richard'd recognize, people whose presence'd be familiar and comforting.

Then there were the rest, all new—at least relatively—to this scene. Mercenary confidence men with no loyalty to the Triad tables, happy to maximize their profits by any means necessary.

These'd been gathered two days earlier and given a set of signals known only to each other. These signals were subtle, easy to remember, and communicated the simplest of information. Information like *I'm bluffing*, or the relative strength of the hand, as denoted by assigning each one a point value. A straight, for example, was assigned a value of four, as it beat three other hands (high card notwithstanding). Once they'd communicated their hands, our actors would decide whether to start betting (if at least one had a high-value hand) or fold (if none did). Naturally, their pots at the end would be totaled and divided evenly among them, just to make sure nobody got the bright idea to backstab the group for the pot. On the other hand, anyone caught signaling improperly lost their share. My actors were bound to my interests with bonds more powerful than oaths—economic incentives.

Some days, it feels like it's you against the entire table. Most of the time, that's not actually the case.

*Most* of the time . . .

Well, it wasn't *all* bad for Richard. He wasn't losing *all* the time, after all—every so often, he lucked into a winning hand. Recent psychological studies, such as those performed by Stephen Kendall on pigeons, suggest that the best way to get people to continue a desirable behavior (in this case, playing poker) is to reward them *intermittently*, i.e., on an unpredictable schedule. The effect is compounded if the reward itself's also random—which explains why slot machines're so addictive to some people.

By this principle, occasionally rewarding Richard with a big win would keep him playing far longer than he would've normally. So occasionally, the colluding players'd run up a nice big pot, then slowly fold, leaving one or two people with weak hands to "lose" to Richard. But a few large wins weren't enough to stem the slow, inexorable bleed—he'd maxed out two credit cards already.

Three hours later, he was out of credit cards.

"I can't just write you a check?" he snapped at Addie, who was doing a masterful job of cowering.

"Checks can bounce, sir," said Addie.

"Bullshit! I'm a rich man; you've seen the kind

of money I'm throwing around. You think that check will bounce?"

"It's not my decision to make, sir."

Richard was exactly as livid as you'd expect someone who's been gradually losing large amounts of money for five or six hours to be. But the Triad hires private security at gambling events to keep temper tantrums under control, and it was after eying them warily that he stepped away from the counter.

"Alright then," he said. "Alright. One moment."

He stepped into a corner outside the mic's range and started talking into a cellphone. I tapped out a quick message to Kira.

You getting it?

A few seconds later came her reply. yup.

What's he doing?

xactly what u said

I smiled triumphantly. "It's all going according to plan," I said to Z. He deliberately ignored me.

Sheesh.

A few minutes later, Richard approached Addie again. "I just wired you fifteen thousand dollars— check if you want."

Addie did so, then bent down to retrieve yet another supply of chips. Richard practically ripped them out of her hands. I kept my eyes on Addie though, watched her pick up her smartphone and slide in a pair of earbuds.

Listening, no doubt, to the audio of Richard's call that Kira'd just sent her. Familiarizing herself with his words, his voice. Z'd been skeptical she could believably imitate him, but she'd insisted she could—and'd imitated Z flawlessly to prove her point.

It was perhaps a half-hour later when she approached the table with a tray of drinks (the attendant behind the counter filled multiple roles). It was hard to see small details on the camera, so I couldn't tell the exact moment her hand slipped into Richard's pocket and retrieved his phone. But when she excused herself from the room under the pretense of a bathroom break, I knew she'd gotten it.

And she had everything she could possibly need. The phone, the voice, and the record of a previous transaction, complete with passwords and security information. All she had to do was redial the number and ask Richard's financial manager to wire another sum of money, this time to one of *our* accounts (in this case, a nice Swiss account I'd opened under a false name *years* ago). How much money would she be withdrawing? Well, that all depended.

On how much there was.

Movies often portray hacking as intensely complicated, involving computers and technical know-how. *Sometimes* that's true, but every *decent* hacker knows the safest, simplest, and most effective way to gain access to secure systems is by fooling the very fallible human in charge of those systems—in this case, the person on the other end of the line.

There was nothing in Addie's face or gait that indicated she'd been successful when she returned—she was far too good an actor for that—but I knew she had. She was competent enough for us both, and when I gave her a job, I could rest easy knowing it'd get done. And that was worth the world to me.

She made a quick stop by the table to "check on the game" (read, return the phone to our unsuspecting mark). This time, as she rested a hand on the table, she tapped it twice—a signal to those who were in on the con. In the coming hands, Richard would find that his luck had begun to turn, and win a few minor hands. The *real* scam was already over, after all.

In the face of Z's continued silence, I turned back to my computer to check on the rest of the moving parts. I'd been notified of the transfer, but it'd take a few hours to roll over fully. That was why it was important to feed Richard a few wins—it'd keep him invested in the game a little longer. If he got back in touch with his financial manager and learned about the money transfer before it was finalized, there was a chance they could cancel it.

Next I checked on Kira. I had a message from her waiting.

my back hurts :( this sux. also bored as shit. nver lisning 2 u EVER AGAIN

That indicated nothing serious'd gone wrong, at least. I replied so she wouldn't complain at me for ignoring her later. You're tough, suck it up.

"Holy shit," I said a few hours later.

Z looked over at me in spite of himself, tiredness rimming his eyes. Dawn was starting to peek over the horizon and the game was winding down. I was dead exhausted—we all were—but there was no sleeping until the plan was finished. Just in case.

"What?" he said.

I turned my computer screen toward him so he could see the specifics of the now-completed wire transfer.

"Holy shit."

I did some quick math. Eighty percent to the Triad, subtract expenses, then divide into quarters . . . That was still almost three million each.

If the Triad hadn't been squeezing us, it would've been significantly more, and I felt a fleeting sadness at the thought.

Z almost smiled, I was sure of it. "You talked up the revenge, dude. Why didn't you mention the sweet, sweet cash?"

"I wanted to surprise you," I grinned. I hadn't *planned* on the take melting Z's frozen heart, but I wasn't gonna pass up opportunities that landed in front of me. Making inroads toward repairing our broken friendship would be a nice bonus on top of my millions. It's rare that a plan's *more* successful than expected, but never unwelcome.

Now was probably a good time to press the issue, since Z seemed more amiable than normal, and we could talk one-on-one. "Dude . . . I'm real sorry about your dad. I never—"

"Whatever," said Z, without letting me finish. "Don't worry about it."

But the nettles were back in his voice, and his body language closed again. I could take a hint, and backed off—cursing my impatience. Rome wasn't built in a day. It could take *months* to dig the stick out of Z's ass.

The game ended by mutual agreement about twenty minutes later—many people had things to do with their Sunday morning. Richard'd "managed" to reverse his fortunes somewhat, ending with forty-three thousand dollars—almost an order of magnitude less than he'd put *in*, but he hadn't needed to withdraw more money since he'd tapped his account, and he was looking pretty proud of himself.

A recent string of successes can dim your memories of past failures to almost nothing. In Richard's eyes, he'd triumphed over his own bad luck. But in the other players' eyes, he'd given them far more than they'd given him.

In our eyes? The game'd never been important.

The players we'd planted made excuses to linger while the rest trickled out. Addie presided as they divvied up their winnings, shook hands, and went their separate ways.

Security was next to go, and now the room was empty save for Addie, who knocked on the countertop to indicate to Kira that it was safe to come out—which she did, haltingly, amid a cloud of invectives, almost doubled over in pain.

"I hope you're still listening," she said into a mic, "Because I want you to hear me say, 'Fuck you,' and I'm never—"

I turned off the sound system. Whether I listened now or not, I'd hear it again later. Besides, I needed quiet to execute the next phase.

Because taking Richard Trieze's money wasn't enough. We'd tried that last time, and he'd set us up to die. A stronger message was called for.

I dialed his number. He picked up on the second ring. "Hello, Richard Trieze speaking."

"Hello," I said in my best villainous drawl. "I hate to be the bearer of bad news, but . . . you're broke."

# TWELVE

**D**EAD SILENCE FROM THE OTHER END. I COUNTED the seconds waiting for Richard's response. *Five . . . six . . .*

"Who is this?" he demanded at last. He hadn't recognized my voice, so that was one automatic fail-state avoided. Disguises're so much easier to maintain over the phone.

That's another thing movies get mostly wrong, by the way. Disguises. Sometimes you get lucky and your mark has some form of face-blindness, but other times you don't. And movie disguises aren't even *good*, I guess so the audience can figure it out. Westley in *Princess Bride*, for example? That robber's mask wouldn't fool Stevie Wonder, much less a devoted ex-girlfriend.

"I'm no one to be trifled with. That is all you need ever know." Of course, now that I was thinking of *Princess Bride*, there's no way I wasn't gonna quote it when an opportunity that good presented itself. Z rolled his eyes. Obviously, he didn't approve of fun.

I could hear Richard breathing, slow and deep, steadying his rhythm before he replied. "That's not an answer."

"Observant of you. I'll be clearer. I'm the man who's almost sixty million dollars richer than he was yesterday. At your expense, naturally."

"You're the—I—what?"

"The money's long gone, of course" I continued, ignoring Richard's pathetic attempts at forming a coherent sentence. "I wouldn't have called if it hadn't been moved and split up several times. The trail is long and well-obscured. Your money's beyond your power to recover."

This was a lie—the money was still in the Swiss bank account Richard's manager'd moved it to. Theoretically, with enough litigation, he could *maybe* get his fortune back, but lawsuits cost money . . . which Richard no longer had. By the time he could marshal his remaining assets and hire a good lawyer, our plan would already be over. And then no lawsuit in the world could help him.

"You'll understand if I check that," said Richard.

"Take your time."

There was a long pause, peppered with clicking. I knew the exact moment he saw I wasn't bullshitting—I heard the intake of breath.

"I've made my point then?"

"I thought the Triad trustworthy," he snapped. "And smart enough to understand the business of hosting games. Unsafe games bleed players, and I'll make sure everyone knows that's all your games are—unsafe. I'll stand on street corners with a billboard if I have to."

"The Triad?" I laughed. A slow, controlled laugh, the kind a predator might make when amusing himself with a choice bit of prey. "I am not the Triad, though it suited me to appear as such. Glad to hear you were taken in. You should be more careful on the phone, Mr. Trieze—you never know who might be listening."

"What do you *want?*" snarled Richard in a tone so heated I swear I saw smoke rising from the receiver.

"Enough money to last until I retire . . . and I already *have* that."

"You called me for a reason."

"I suppose I did," I sighed. And then I hit *record* on the computer software I had open.

It was the same software Kira'd used to record Richard's earlier call. She'd set everything up on my laptop before she left with Addie and told me all I needed to do was hit the button. The few trial runs'd gone perfectly, so I assumed it was working now. Assumed and *hoped*—I didn't wanna have to break into NSA's servers for a recording.

Though I *would,* if I had to. This call was *that* fucking important.

"Here's the deal, Mr. Trieze. You represent one of five wealthy business owners who are known to deal in less explicitly legal ventures. All of you were targeted tonight with the intent of catching your attention. You have skills, Trieze, skills I was confident we could secure if we held your fortune hostage. The local Mafia is moving a large quantity of heroin across state lines into Virginia within the next two weeks, in violation of the Gambino family's prohibition. However, I do *not* know the specifics of when and where the shipment will be moved. I need someone to find out, then secure the shipment in a way that does not immediately alert the Mafia that something's gone wrong . . . and that cannot be traced back to me, of course. The heroin will then be delivered to a location that I will specify later."

I stopped and let the silence build until Richard realized he was expected to talk.

"I do that job, I get my money back?"

"I'm glad we understand each other," I said smugly. "Of course, we don't need all five of you. Whoever best convinces me they can do the job will have the opportunity to prove himself and regain his money. The other four, well . . . you built your fortunes once. You can do it again."

"I see," said Richard, voice like an iced-over lake. "And it's expected that we do this *without* the money we'd normally have access to?"

"Let us assume, for the moment, that that's the case. What other assets could you draw upon?"

Richard thought for a few seconds. Then, "My name is not unknown among my associates. Its strength would do for credit. In my years on the other side of the law, I've come to know the best in the business—or close to it. All their expertise would be at my fingertips."

"A glorified liaison, then?" I snorted. "Surely you can do better than *that*."

"I don't really understand what I'm supposed to—"

"Well, why didn't you *say so*, Trieze? Let me reduce it to more simple terms. You give me reasons to choose you. Good, unique reasons, not this *I know people* bullshit."

Upon saying this, I gave Z an apologetic look, as if to say, *present company excepted.*

A few more seconds of thinking. "I've been heroin-free my whole life. I won't be tempted to double-cross you for the product."

"*That's* more like it," I said. But he was hovering around what I needed to hear. "What else?"

"I'm careful," Richard tried. "Sounds like you want this job to go smoothly. I promise you, I don't make foolish mistakes."

I was beginning to get fed up with Richard's slowness, so I decided to help him along. "And you think you can fool the Mafia?"

Richard chuckled, and in that moment, I caught a glimpse of the old, clownlike Richard—the public face he presented. "Friend, I was fooling the Mafia fresh out of college. Their honor code makes them easy to predict."

"Big talk." I let a layer of condescension creep into my voice.

"Deservedly so," said Richard. "Take earlier this year, for example. I had some people giving me trouble. A gang of crooks. They messed with me, and my hands were tied dealing with them. So I got them hired by the mob."

"And what happened?" I said, though I already knew.

"They fell for it. Did the job the mob wanted. But I made it look like they'd betrayed the mob in the process. Financially benefited where they shouldn't have. So the mob took care of them the way they do—permanently. That was the end of that."

And there it was, out in the open.

I'd been sure, of course. I wouldn't have come to Washington otherwise. But being sure was one thing, and *knowing* was another.

Richard Trieze had fed us to the Mafia. Deliberately. In the hope that we'd die at their hands.

He'd left four large bets on the basketball game we'd rigged, made to look like we were breaking our deal, betraying our employers. Just to increase the chances we'd be killed.

It was a move right out of Lucas's playbook. And that's when I decided he deserved whatever he got. Any doubts about my current path died there, in that revelation.

Another thought, less important but not unnoticed: Richard didn't know we'd survived. Hadn't bothered to check thoroughly, anyway. Maybe the Vegas Mafia'd told him their men were successful. Maybe he'd just assumed.

Either way, it was a mistake he wouldn't get to make twice.

"You're very well acquainted with how the Mafia operates," I said.

Richard knew a lifeline when he saw one. "It's a particular strength of mine. For this job, I'd say it's a skill you can't go without."

That was enough. I had what I needed.

"You've made quite the case for yourself, Mr. Trieze," I said. "We'll be in touch. Don't call us—we'll call *you*."

With one small movement of my thumb, I ended the call. Then I stopped the recording. The sound file expanded and prompted me to name it.

Z's eyes were boring into the back of my head.

"You got what you want," he said, indicating the computer.

I didn't respond. But it was an obvious *yes*.

"We're really gonna do this."

"We don't have a choice."

Z shook his head. "There's always a choice. And you're making it."

The weight of his disapproval pressed against

my chest with palpable force. And yet, he'd gone along with the plan. Helped us through the early stages. He'd kinda missed the boat to be objecting *now*. But that's how Z *always* operated. He condemned our methods from the sidelines, paying lip service to his morality while helping us regardless.

But I didn't need his approval. Just his assistance.

# THIRTEEN

L A COSA NOSTRA WAS AN UPSCALE ITALIAN BISTRO in Columbia Heights. In many ways, it was your average restaurant—moderately luxurious (though time-worn) accommodations, pictures of the owner on the wall, lattice-work black metal tables under an awning outside to increase its capacity.

It was *unusual* in that it was a front for the Washington, DC, Mafia.

"Really?" Addie rolled her eyes. "'La Cosa Nostra'? They aren't even trying to be subtle."

I was with her on that. I almost suspected that the restaurant was just trying to make money off the mob's image. But Z'd insisted this was the seat of Mafia power in Washington, DC, to the extent that they had any. "Heard it straight from a friend," he'd said when pressed, and we'd stopped questioning him then, because asking Z for more details about his friends leads to boring stories about how they met. Nobody has time for that shit.

"You think they'll know our faces?" I asked, and he'd shaken his head.

"We aren't that big a deal. They'd know us in New York, but not here."

I wasn't convinced. We had, after all, been part of the chain of events that'd kicked off a new anti-crime wave in New York. Depending on how much the Mafia attributed that to us, it could be that every family in the country knew our names and faces. But Z seemed sure, and I was trying to get back on his good side.

Besides, say we walked into La Cosa Nostra and they recognized us. What were they gonna do, shoot us dead? For ordering a slice of pizza? In broad daylight, surrounded by witnesses? No, it was probably safe to come in whether they recognized us or not.

"Don't take any stupid risks," I said to Addie, handing her the flash drive.

"Smart risks only. Got it," she said, then smiled to show she was joking. "Kiss for luck?"

I obliged her, and Kira gagged. "Jesus Christ, I'm vomiting kittens over here." Addie flipped her off.

"See you guys soon," she said. I couldn't find an excuse to delay, so I turned, beckoning with my head for the others to follow.

It was peak lunch hour, as evidenced by the crowded tables. We'd timed things pretty well—an overworked staff was advantageous to us. Luckily, they had enough room to squeeze us in near the center of the dining area, squished up against four other tables. Nobody was looking at us suspiciously, or talking to a supervisor while pointing in our direction, or pulling out a semiautomatic and shooting at us, so I figured we were safe.

Ten minutes after we sat down, a waiter brought us water, and promptly disappeared without taking any orders. Normally, I'd have been annoyed at that level of inefficiency, but the lack of interruption was in this case preferable. Besides, they were having a busy day—I could cut the staff some slack.

Addie showed up about six minutes later, looking apologetic. "Sorry," she said, sitting down. "It's just not happening—they've got the back area locked down."

I was skeptical. "You can't sneak past a few guards? I'm having trouble believing that."

"Sneaking past them, no problem. I wasn't caught or anything. But the boss's office is shut tight, with two guys keeping watch right in front. There aren't any other entrances, not even windows—I looked. There's hard, and there's impossible."

Her statement was made with some measure of defensiveness, and I backpedaled. "Not blaming you. Okay, so security's better than we expected. We'll just go with plan B."

Unfortunately, I'd only planned as far as plan A.

"We have a plan B?" said Kira.

"It really *was* impossible," Addie pressed. "There was no way to open that door without people noticing."

I looked at her, amused. "You're too used to succeeding, aren't you?"

Addie scowled.

I slid some paper and a pen out of my pocket and started jotting down notes, occasionally asking Addie what she'd seen while she was snooping. Not attempting to solve the problem, just listing constraints, goals, and obstacles.

(On a side note, carrying paper and a pen with you everywhere you go costs you little and can be *very* useful in a wide range of situations. I suggest getting into the habit.)

Once I felt satisfied with my outline of the problem, I began generating ideas. The best of these made it onto the paper, where they became subject to edits or deletion. It was tough ignoring Z's complaints about the menu, but I'm used to ignoring him in general, which helped.

The waiter returned during this time and I stopped working long enough to order the pasta primavera. I didn't bother hiding my work—it was a mess of scribbles entirely indecipherable to outside observers.

Finally, I had what looked like a workable plan, one which operated within the constraints to thwart the obstacles and deliver the goal. Not my simplest, but they can't *all* be as perfect as me.

"Okay," I said, and everyone looked at me expectantly. "Addie, you'll be posing as a Mafiosa. You take Z into the back and tell the guards you caught him snooping. Then—"

"Hold the fuck up," said Z. "What?"

"It'll be safe," I promised. "Kira will step in to save your ass if—"

"Nope," said Z. "Not happening. I get screwed over every single plan you make, and this is just *begging* to go wrong. Change the plan."

"I can't—"

"Not gonna do it. Change the fucking plan."

I sighed and turned my eyes back to the paper.

So Z was unwilling to play the part of the snoop. How could I incorporate that wrinkle into the plan without wrecking it? Perhaps . . .

A few more minutes of scratching at the paper, to no avail. "Hey, are you sure—"

"Fuck. You."

He was sure.

I stared at my sheet of paper, now more black than white, and *willed* a solution out of the different elements I'd outlined . . . and realized abruptly that I was being stupid. That there was a simple, foolproof plan that cut away the constraints and obstacles with barely any effort needed, if I just approached the problem from the perspective of an average person without access to a team of talented individuals.

"Okay," I said again. "This one's *tons* better. Kira, go buy me some envelopes."

"But my food—"

"—Isn't gonna get here before you come back. This service is slower than Mr. McCallister grading assignments."

Kira started to get up, but paused, looking conflicted.

"The longer you wait, the less chance you'll get back in time."

She went.

"This plan seems pretty different from the last one," said Addie.

I shrugged. "It's the kind that'd never make it into a heist movie for being both too effective and utterly boring to watch. Can you find the host and read his name off the tag? Don't let him see you."

"No problem."

I looked at my notes, searching for a margin of white space large enough to contain a little more writing. "Hey Z. Your friend told you this was the DC Mafia's base of operations. Did he mention the boss's name?"

Z wrinkled his brow, trying to remember. "Yeah,

uh . . . Leone something. Pon, Pon . . . Ponzio. That's it, Leone Ponzio."

I squeezed the name between a Bayesian probability estimate and a rough schematic of the restaurant, then circled it. "Thanks. Got any twenties? I'll pay you back."

Z looked at me for a moment, trying to figure out why a guy worth millions would need to borrow money in double-digit denominations.

"It's been kinda rough since you left."

Wordlessly, he dug two bills out of his wallet and slid them across the table.

Addie returned. "His name's Walter Ercole," she reported, and this too I wrote down.

"So, what's the plan?" asked Z.

"All in due time," I promised. Withholding information until a dramatic reveal's one of my great joys in life. "Let's wait for Kira."

When Kira got back, I was digging into my pasta primavera while her *bistecca* slowly cooled next to me.

"Goddammit," she growled, shoving a box of envelopes into my hands.

"Be faster next time," I replied with a grin, and she kicked me under the table. I yelped and rubbed my stinging leg.

"So, plan?" asked Z around a mouthful of bread.

"One sec," I said, opening the package of envelopes. "Addie, gimme the stuff."

Addie handed over the flash drive I'd given her, which was now wrapped inside a note. This I took and sealed inside the first envelope. On it, I wrote *Leone Ponzio* in big letters, and beneath that, *Manager, La Cosa Nostra*.

I set this envelope aside and picked up a second. On this one, I wrote:

*Walter Ercole*
*Staff, La Cosa Nostra Restaurant*
*Monroe St., Columbia Heights*

Then, I placed the first envelope inside, along with the money Z'd given me.

I drummed my fingers on the table, stalling for time. This was my last chance to turn back. Would I regret not taking it?

My resolve solidified.

"Here," I said, handing the envelope-within-an-envelope to Addie. "Go give this to Mr. Ercole. Tell him you received an envelope with your name on it, and that this was inside."

I'd thought of several similar solutions when brainstorming, but discarded them due to the necessity of one of us showing ourselves to the intermediary. But if Addie passed herself off as just another unassuming link in the chain, beneath suspicion, that worry no longer applied.

Addie took the envelope and left again. I took a piece of her garlic bread while she was gone.

"The plan?" said Z again. God, but he was persistent.

"All done," I said. "That was it."

Z blinked, and Kira burst out laughing.

"What?" I said. "It didn't have to be complicated."

"You were gonna have Addie *turn me in as a spy* instead of just doing *that*?"

"At any rate," I said, ignoring Z, "the plan moves forward now . . . with or without our help."

Z grew suddenly serious. "Dammit, Jason. This is a bad idea. I was gonna talk you out of it. I was . . . I didn't think the plan'd be so *quick*—"

"You wouldn't have succeeded," I said shortly. I didn't wanna talk about it. Z's dark eyes smoldered and I felt the tension between us again, taut like a bowstring.

I couldn't blame him for disagreeing—I'd *known* he would. I'd surprised even myself coming up with it. It was unlike any plan I'd ever made, and not in a good way.

"It might not work," I offered, but I knew it was a poor excuse. You don't make plans if you want them to fail.

# FOURTEEN

SOMETHING'D SAPPED THE AIR OF ITS HEAT, LEAVING it soggy and tepid against my skin. Unusual, for a summer night. The gray clouds masking the sky would've been better suited for November.

The air was charged, too, like the weather was trying hard to add lightning into the mix and not *quite* getting there. But lightning or no, just feeling the buildup was unnerving all the same.

The atmosphere held its breath. The calm before the storm.

And somewhere beyond my comprehension, events were playing out. Events I'd set in motion, and could no longer stop. Even if I'd wanted to.

We stood huddled on a DC sidewalk, binoculars pointed fruitlessly at a house two long blocks down from our position. I say fruitlessly because the night made vision difficult. Dim streetlamps fought the gloom with their orange, florescent glow as best they could, but they might as well've been burnt out for all the good they did.

Our lawmakers spent so much time arguing, they couldn't even pass a resolution to change the bulbs in their own city.

That was the kind of observation that jokes were made of, and any other time I would've cracked one. But there was an uneasy silence about the group, an unspoken contract that grew more and more binding the longer we all respected it. The silence'd held for three hours and counting, and that contract was practically written in stone by now.

Not that there wasn't anything to discuss. Quite the contrary, in fact—there was too much. That was the problem.

We didn't have to be here. There was no reason

for it. But I'd insisted. I felt it was owed, on some cosmological level, to see what results our actions wrought. Because there's a word for people who ignore the consequences of their actions. You know what we call them? Kids.

And despite what our opponents always say, usually while laughing, we aren't kids. Not anymore. Not after today, even if we had been before.

We were closing in on four hours of silent waiting when . . .

"Maybe they ain't coming."

I started. Kira swore. Only Addie seemed unaffected by the sudden intrusion of words into our collective quiet. I would've forgotten she was here by now if she weren't holding tight to my hand—she would've found a shadow and slipped into it.

"They're coming," I said. "Maybe not today, but they are."

I wasn't sure how long I was willing to keep up this silent vigil. Four hours was annoying, but I'd suffer through it. But would I still be here *twelve* hours from now? Forty-eight? We'd have to start taking shifts.

"Newsflash, Jason. Your plans don't gotta work one hundred percent of the time. Maybe this time something went wrong. They thought it wasn't worth it, didn't wanna risk their position, anything."

I didn't react to Z's goading. I didn't wanna drive him further away.

"Maybe you gotta get your hands dirty for once if you want it so bad," taunted Z. His voice was low to avoid attracting attention, but I could hear every word plainly. "But it's not that easy, huh? You got no problem giving the order, but—"

"Z," said Addie coldly. "Shut up."

To my surprise, he did. He gave one last contemptuous snort, then turned away, back toward the house we were watching. I think it was mostly surprise at Addie's venom that did it. She wasn't immune to anger—I would know—but she always kept it on lockdown regardless of how she felt. This was as close as I'd ever seen her to flying off the handle.

And it'd been in my defense. Under different circumstances, I'd be over the moon.

Addie squeezed my hand. "Don't worry," she muttered into my ear. "You're making the right call."

But when I put down the binoculars and looked back at her, she wouldn't meet my eyes.

What did she want from me? To take it back? I couldn't do that. To've decided differently, at some point in the past? Well, it wasn't any more my fault than hers. I'd come up with the plan, I'd given the orders, but my will wasn't law. She could've refused at any time, called me out. I'd have listened.

Even Z, for all his posturing, was just as culpable as I was. He'd set up the meeting with the Triad, told us where the Mafia was. He'd done it knowing the plan. And now he was standing right next to us on the sidewalk, watching.

Only Kira seemed relatively unbothered. Sure,

she wasn't talking, which was rare. But if I had to guess, I'd say she was just doing it to fit in with us, respecting the group dynamic.

Which, now that I thought about it, was *also* out of character . . .

Kira was relaxed, at ease. She wasn't treating me differently like the others. She'd been the first of them to endorse this plan—onboard since the beginning.

And now I'd noticed her keeping a close eye on the group dynamic and mimicking it, trying to fit in. This was . . . not at all like Kira's previous interactions with the group. Almost the *opposite* of what I'd come to expect.

Then again, Kira actively hid her criminal activities from her family. What was that but a reaction to *that* group dynamic?

I had to update my priors to accommodate the possibility that she was *much* better at reading social situations than I'd ever given her credit for.

And if *that* were true . . . maybe she was a better *actor* than she let on too.

Meaning . . .

Something clicked, observations and patterns and evidence falling in line to form a complete picture.

Only one sequence of events fits every observation, and that's reality. If observations appear contradictory, you haven't found reality yet.

Conversely, when at last you stumble upon the correct conclusion, everything aligns perfectly, fits into place like the pieces of an interlocking metal cube puzzle, suddenly so obvious you can't believe you didn't realize sooner.

Kira didn't just like fighting. She liked to hurt people.

And she hid that truth behind a love of fighting, because she knew it was socially unacceptable. The same way she hid that same love of fighting from her family behind a veneer of normality. Because she was socially conscious in a way we'd never realized.

And she'd wrestled with her inclination, tried to conquer it. She'd thanked me in Vegas for suggesting a plan where she didn't have to fight. She'd bailed on the bar fight on the off-chance she'd have to step in. It wasn't, as I'd assumed, some strange new pacifistic streak. It was the exact opposite, a desire to harm so strong it scared her. And somewhere down the line, she'd simply given up.

And, *and*, she'd *lied* about what went down at Addie's house during the mob raid. Addie and I hadn't given that much thought after we'd dug up the truth. But *was* it the truth, really? The news reports'd all quoted Isabella Mendez's rendition of events, so now that I thought about it, Addie and I *hadn't* gotten corroborating stories from multiple sources—they'd come from the same place.

That version of the story had four men. Kira's had had three.

*Why* change the number?

Why, unless she'd said the real number without thinking? If there *had* been three, they couldn't have all killed each other simultaneously—you needed a fourth. But who could contradict her if she *claimed* there'd been a fourth?

I'd assumed she'd been trying to hide that she'd been too scared to fight. Maybe it was the opposite—she'd been too eager. But she'd known that in a fight against three trained killers, there'd be no "scaring them off". She'd have had to catch them by surprise, and go for the kill.

*Go for the kill.*

And there she was now, standing nonchalantly next to Z like she was waiting for her mom to pick her up. Like she didn't care that odds were she was about to watch herself become complicit in a murder.

There was suddenly something very *sinister* about the way she was holding those binoculars . . .

I leaned down to whisper what I'd just realized to Addie. But then I reconsidered. This wasn't the kind of talk you have when the person you're talking about is standing just feet away. There'd be time later, when we could talk freely without drawing suspicion, when we could spare the mental energies to really think through the implications, no longer preoccupied with our current situation.

So I turned the whisper into sort of a nuzzle against her neck instead. She snuggled closer to me and I felt some of the tension leave her.

So she didn't think I was a *total* monster, at least.

That helped, in its way. Like, as long as Addie cared about me, I hadn't lost myself. I guess it's stupid, but I'm sure there's someone you feel that way about. Someone whose opinion you value, whose disapproval's enough to make you reconsider your choices.

Or not. I dunno.

The two of us stayed that way some time longer, leaning against each other. And then . . .

"Headlights," said Addie, pointing.

Sure enough, two bright yellow headlights were advancing up the road, cutting through the night like twin scalpels. We took an instinctive step backward, into the shadows. Being seen could be bad.

Through the binoculars, I watched as the car parked, two blocks down. The headlights darkened, leaving only the orangish glow of the streetlamps. And then three men stepped out of the car, leaving a fourth behind the wheel.

I heard a sharp breath to my right. Z's fists were clenched at his sides. They seemed frozen in place. His jaw was set, his lips pressed together so hard the color was draining from them.

He was, I realized, watching the exact same sequence of events that'd led to his father's death.

Before I raised my binoculars again, I took a quick look at the other two. Addie was expression-less, relaxed, same as always—and, same as always, I couldn't tell what she was thinking. She looked like a scientist observing animals in the wild. Kira was leaned forward with a predatory, *hungry* look on her face, and it shocked me all over again that I hadn't noticed before.

I looked back at the house just in time to watch the men file in. It was almost midnight. Most adults would already be in bed, not suspecting anything was amiss . . .

And the wrongness of what was about to happen hit me like a frying pan. This wasn't right. I opened my mouth to shout a warning—and whatever part of my brain was responsible for recognizing *stupid fucking ideas* slammed it shut again. Noise wouldn't help. It'd only draw their attention. My mind raced, trying to find a plan, watching the three men as they moved onto the front porch and started fiddling with the lock. But of course, I'd planned too well—taken into account even my own potential squeamishness, leaving me with no countermeasures past a certain point. I would've needed the power to go back in time and call the whole thing off, and that, I didn't possess.

I'd known, deep down, that I wasn't a killer. And so I'd passed the responsibility off to another, with nothing but a flash drive and a hastily drafted note, typed and printed to hide my handwriting. The drive, of course, had contained the sound file of the conversation between Richard and myself. The note, wrapped around it, was self-explanatory.

*The man who admits to using you is named Richard Trieze. The business associates he mentions did not die at your hands—they survived and sought revenge against La Cosa Nostra. As a direct result of their actions, New York City began its recent crackdown on Mafia-associated businesses and figures. All because Richard Trieze thought he could use you for his own ends.*

*Richard Trieze lives at 5155 Rockwood Parkway in Kent, Washington, DC. He lives alone.*

*Highest regards,*
*A friend and ally*

It was, in retrospect, a fairly obvious bit of manipulation. But it was the kind of manipulation where even if you recognize it, you still have no choice but to go along with it. The Mafia was a proud organization with a strict code of honor, and humiliations on the level that Richard'd brought upon them were punishable in very specific ways. You didn't just *not* punish him because someone else obviously *wanted* you to . . .

But all the arguments I'd used to talk myself into it, all the reasons why Richard *had* to die, they all seemed so false now. There were *dozens* of other options. Less sure, perhaps—but perhaps that lack of surety would've been worth it.

Two loud cracks in quick succession split the night. Then a third.

Lights started turning on up and down the street. We couldn't afford to wait around. So we exchanged quiet looks and retreated down the street into darkness.

# FIFTEEN

NEEDLESS TO SAY, WE DIDN'T STAY IN DC MUCH longer—just long enough to finish our business with the Triad. We were anxious to leave the city behind.

The drive home was possibly the most awkward drive ever. It was mostly silence, with a few lame attempts at conversation that died ignobly due to lack of interest. I think we all just wanted time to think things over, process the uncomfortable truths this trip'd revealed—about ourselves *and* each other. Needless to say, there wouldn't be much of a Revel this time around.

I've never been more grateful that Kira was our

driver. She was the least affected of us all, and while she still buzzed the usual amount of cars on the highway, it was the safe, comfortable kind of chaos that comes with the territory, and not the kind that involves crashing into the center divider because we were too lost in thought to watch the road. If I'd been driving, we might not've made it back without an accident.

For once, seeing the gates of my house was a relief. Even facing Lucas (*the man who maybe wanted me dead*, I reminded myself) was preferable to staying in that quiet, uncertain car one minute longer. We agreed to meet and debrief tomorrow, which at least gave me a whole night alone with my thoughts. Also literally alone, because Lucas was out on some business trip and Jeeves was covering his duties.

So I took the opportunity to snoop through Lucas's desktop, hidden behind three levels of access codes I bypassed like they weren't even there. I'd known the aging computer's password (potentiaestrex) since I was twelve, and I was hoping he'd left some answers lying around.

I *had* to know his game. How much danger I was in just living here.

There was nothing of relevance among the gigabytes of financial records, outlines of future projects, and compilations of blackmail material for various local politicians. Nothing but a folder innocuously labeled *Jason Jorgensen*, hidden as an invisible icon.

The folder was encrypted. Unlike every other file.

Who knows how many answers lay hidden within that folder that I couldn't read. I tried every trick in my limited repertoire, then stared at it for several minutes tingling with curiosity and frustration.

I could've called Kira and asked her to help, but I didn't wanna talk to her right now. So I did something I don't often do—gave up. Turned the computer off and went to bed, feeling defeated. And worried.

And so, with the covers pulled up around me, I

lost myself to musing. At first, I tried distracting my mind by thinking about the thirty Gs sitting in my bank account and what it could buy, but I couldn't stop dwelling on who that money'd belonged to originally, and what'd happened to him. So I shut down that line of thought cold and instead asked myself, *where do we go from here?* Because I didn't see how the CPC could continue to operate under the current circumstances.

Z hated me. And not the convenient kind of hatred, where it burns so hot and intense that it puffs out sadly if you take pains not to feed it. No, his was a cold, assured disdain that wouldn't be worn down overnight—or perhaps even in a month. But he wouldn't be sticking around, so maybe that didn't matter. My name was shit with a lot of people—what was one more?

Kira was sadistic, and while I didn't know the extent of her inclinations, I knew it was enough that she knew she had to hide it—and that wasn't a good sign. And if she'd hidden that side of herself from us . . . what else was she hiding? What would she do if she lost control? The potential answers scared me, but the questions themselves were scary in their own right.

Addie was hiding something from me. She'd always had secrets—hell, that was part of what made her so attractive—but it felt . . . different, when one involved me personally. That secret was giving me doubts, getting into my head, distracting me. Nothing like the idea of Addie's secrets *in the abstract*, which manifested as a mischievous glint in her green eyes and could be unraveled at my leisure.

And as if suddenly distrusting my three team-mates wasn't enough, I couldn't even rely on the one guy I'd always counted on . . . me.

"The only person you can trust is yourself," was another fatherly piece of advice Lucas gave me when I was growing up. Of course, he'd said this right after *not* buying me the movie ticket he'd said he'd buy me if I cleaned the kitchen. It's a wonder I didn't grow up to be a psychopath. But I digress—back to the nature of trust, or lack thereof.

Lucas'd been of the opinion that I *could* trust myself, and I'd never seen a reason *not* to—until my past self overrode my moral sense and set the plan so my future self couldn't counter it. If it'd been someone else, I'd already have countermeasures in place for the next time it happened. But it hadn't been someone else—just me.

*I'd* given those orders, not some alien "past self". And any countermeasures I could dream up, I could circumvent.

What a group of fuckups we were.

And that last thought, echoing in my mind, accompanied me to sleep.

When I woke up, the magical answer fairy'd failed to visit in the night. But I did feel slightly better, having that much more distance from the event.

I ate a quick breakfast, made small talk with Jeeves, then called my driver. I had an appointment for an eleven a.m. debrief at Kira's to keep, and no amount of misgivings about my teammates were an excuse to keep them waiting.

By the time I pulled up, I was ready to face the team like everything was normal. Addie'd see through my facade in seconds, but she'd also have the sense to keep quiet about it until we were alone. Kira'd see the intelligent, witty, devilishly handsome natural-born leader she was accustomed to seeing.

I didn't consider what Z'd think because I wasn't expecting him to be there. The job was over, and debriefs were more of a duty than anything. He'd made up dozens of excuses to skip them while he was *in* the CPC, so I figured, since he now had the excuse to end all excuses, he'd definitely take the opportunity to not show up. I was surprised when I walked up the stairs to Kira's room and found him sprawled on a large green beanbag. He nodded at me, acknowledging my presence, but didn't say anything.

"Hey," I said, trying my best to cover my surprise.

" 'Sup," said Kira, who was lying face down on her bed. "So I guess this is happening?"

She rolled over onto her side, grimacing. "Next time we schedule a debrief, can we make it a sensible time, when people are actually awake?"

"It's *eleven in the morning.*"

"The point stands."

"She lay down when she heard your car pull up," said Z, who'd apparently decided talking to me was okay after all.

Kira glared at him. Then she grabbed a can of Monster off her bedside table and rocked it next to her ear. The result convinced her to shift her glare to the can instead.

"So we're waiting on Addie?" I asked.

"Yep," said Kira. She whipped the can at my head suddenly and I shielded myself with both arms. The can bounced off my elbow onto the ground.

"Toss that shit in the trash," she said.

I did, not letting her know my arm was stinging. I wasn't gonna give her whatever satisfaction knowing that might've given her. I wasn't sure that made sense in a short-term utility equation, but it was definitely—well, probably—the right move in the long game.

"You're welcome," I said, taking my seat on the toy chest.

"Oh, yeah," said Kira, sitting up. "Z's gonna join up again. He missed us too much."

For the second time that minute I had to cover my surprise. I'd just *assumed* Z would be out the moment the job ended, on account of him hating my guts, and not trusting my moral judgments to align with his.

. . . No, I still *very much* believed that. Kira was joking, or mistaken, or . . .

"The multi-million dollar bonus didn't hurt," said Z sheepishly as I stared at him in shock. "Kira said it was cool. It's cool, right?"

"It's cool," my mouth said on autopilot as my brain tried to reconcile my mental model of Z with reality. Was . . . was he being *nice* to me?

Then I saw his eyes flicker toward Kira, saw her beam back a smile I could only describe as *flirty*, which was such an un-Kira action that my brain almost overloaded before it realized what was happening and reorganized its mental models.

Holy shit. Kira knew Z had a thing for her.

I know *I* hadn't told her. I was ninety percent confident *Addie* hadn't told her. And *he* certainly hadn't given a tear-drenched confession outside her window with a boom box. Which left only one possibility—she'd figured it out herself.

She wasn't supposed to have that much social acumen.

I looked at her with the question written on my face and she winked, which confirmed my suspicions. She'd figured out Z had a crush, started flirting with him, and convinced him to rejoin the group despite his misgivings.

Again, that was *not* the kind of planning I've come to expect from Kira, whose usual plans tend to devolve into throwing punches by step two.

And this was right on the heel of discovering how easily and fully she'd hidden her sadism from the world. Learning that her brash-toughie attitude wasn't the real Kira, just another mask, like the dutiful, straight-laced daughter she presented as around her family, or the gossip-driven prep she pretended to be at school.

How badly had I underestimated Kira Applewood?

"There something on my face?"

I looked down, realizing I'd been staring at Kira for a weird length of time. Hopefully my expression hadn't given anything away.

"Yeah, that stupid smug look 'cause you know you did good," I said. "Welcome back, dude."

"Just don't make me regret this," said Z. He said it jokingly, but the threat was clear. I didn't respond. Didn't know how.

"So," he said, spreading his hands wide. "Kira's been filling me in—tell me if she missed anything.

We're rich, nobody's messing with us, and we got nothing else to worry about."

Except each other. "Sounds like she covered everything. You picked a pretty good time to come back."

"It's p. dope," grinned Kira. "Thinking about getting a new ride. You guys wanna be driven around in a Porsche?"

Z whistled. "I might never use my license again."

"A *new* ride?" I asked. "What about your horse? Is he not good enough?"

Kira smiled so happily at the mention of that horse, I almost forgot she was anything but a normal teenage girl. "Summer Disaster's *great* . . . but he's a one-horsepower vehicle."

"Course, I could always get my own, with all the dough I'm rolling in," mused Z. "Porsche, I mean. Can our next job get us this much cash too?"

Kira shrugged. "That's Jason's job. Whatcha got for us, Jace?"

The honest answer was "nothing," but I didn't

wanna admit that. Having plans was my *thing*. I blew some air out of my mouth to stall, then opened it, still blanking . . .

Luckily, Addie saved me from my plan-less embarrassment by choosing that moment to arrive. Or possibly she'd chosen to arrive some moments earlier and I'd only just noticed. But the moment I saw her, something burst within me, a desire for answers that suddenly couldn't wait until after the meeting, even if I'd originally planned to.

"Hi," I said, taking her by the hand and pulling slightly toward the door. "Can we talk a sec? Outside?"

"Sure," she said, obviously confused, but following my halfhearted tugs while Kira made wet kissing noises at our backs.

I didn't stop until there were three doors between us and Kira's room. We ended up in a guest bedroom, small and only lightly furnished. I closed the door and sat on the bed, which was the only piece of furniture in the room suitable for sitting on.

Several swallows later, I still couldn't get the words out. My throat was rebelling, trying to keep me from starting what could rapidly turn into the Breakup Talk if things went badly.

The bed sank as Addie sat too, and looked at me inquisitively. So I took one last deep breath, convinced my vocal cords that this talk *had to happen*, and said the first thing on my mind.

"I noticed you weren't meeting my eyes when . . . well, you know."

Judging by Addie's face, that *wasn't* what she'd been expecting.

"I dunno if you'll ever see me the same way—" I paused and began again. Nothing sounded right anymore. "I've thought a lot about it and I, I won't make that mistake ag—"

"No," said Addie, putting a reassuring hand on my shoulder. "No, you can't second-guess yourself like that."

I almost choked on whatever words I'd been planning to say next.

"What you did was *right*," Addie said firmly. She was staring straight into my eyes, face drawn and determined. "It wasn't an easy call to make, but you *have* to believe it was the right one."

"Then why, why . . . ?"

"Why couldn't I look at you?" finished Addie. As if saying it reminded her, she tilted her head slightly, breaking our connection. Still looking at me, but not *at* me. "It's not you, it's me."

I flinched back and she caught herself. "Not like that. I promise that's not a precursor to a breakup or anything. I just mean I have some issues to work through—"

"Just like everyone else in this goddamned group." I couldn't help myself. But Addie laughed in spite of herself.

"And I can deal with them myself," she continued. "But I promise, I *will* work them out. And I'm not going to make you wait for me, or anything like that—just in case you were worried."

I managed a tiny smile that wasn't at all

proportional to my rush of relief that it wasn't becoming one of *those* conversations. "Maybe a little."

"Sorry, but you're stuck with me," said Addie. And then she leaned in and hugged me with everything she had, sagging like she'd been storing up every emotion she'd ever felt and not put on display and was now releasing them into me. I half supported her and half sagged myself as some of the stress and turmoil of the last few days leaked away.

"I don't know how things are going to go," said Addie into my shoulder. "But I want to face them with you."

I didn't know either, but right then, it all seemed unimportant. Let Z fill the air between us with ice. Let Kira hide her lunacy from the world. Let Lucas plot against me with all the ruthlessness generally reserved for bitter enemies. I had Addie, Addie had me, and we'd face the world together.

Z and Kira would be waiting a good long while before we rejoined them.